Guiding the Stars

A Boom Generation series

Kelly Fields

kelthscreations.blog

Catherine Fields - editor
Diana Cojocaru – cover art
Daniela Vasquez – inside and cover art

Other books by Kelly Fields
Avant-garde
Millennium Earth
Crossing Rivers

ISBN: 978-0-9998820-3-0

Preface

Weddings are happening on Millennium. Ships are being built for a long journey. The Earth is new with many dangers to be found. Our explorers are going there to try the plan again. A new High Councilor there will be and some new creatures are seen. The old ways are rejected for a time and some will separate. Later Brenda dreams and seems to awaken in her dreams. A new generation is born and there is much to be learned. Earth is filled with strife and the councilors will do their best to maintain the peace. Another marriage will happen that will change the world again. The former High Councilors are together in the end, but their lives are very different.

Guiding the Stars

Athena, Jillela and Coretta
By Daniela Vasquez

CHAPTER 1

Memories are always popping up and this time they would be a beautiful one for Margo. Not that they usually aren't beautiful and thinking about her granddaughter getting married took her back to Earth in the early seventies. She then stopped her mind and heart from going there and said to herself "I want to first share this with Jenny, Tamla, Shasha and Brenda."

Well they were, all there with her! She and Jenny are working on teaching Tamla, Shasha and Brenda some in depth knowledge about politics. Putting her arm around her best friend and confidant for all these years Margo said "Jenny my dear we need to take the girls out somewhere for a long lunch."

"Sounds like a great idea and what place do you have in mind?"

Listening in very attentively on her answer was Shasha, Brenda and Tamla.

"Let's go to our favorite place over by the lake. There, we will all reminisce about our beautiful wedding day."

Brenda smiled sheepishly and said "but I don't have one of those...YET!"

Since they were still in their quarters at the Assembly they all had to keep down their laughter, of how Brenda said that. And they all grabbed their stuff and headed out to the bus to take them to their favorite little Bistro by the lake. Even though the weather on Millennia wasn't perfect anymore this was still a very nice day to be outside.

This little Bistro had gazebos outside for private conversations, in one of them the girls sat down, ordered some wine, cheese, and a loaf of French bread.

"Okay ladies who should start?"

Jenny said "you should Margo after all you were married first."

The rest just nodded got quiet and poured some wine, sliced the bread and cheese then settled in.

"Sure, I was thinking about this today and started to reminisce about my wedding and marrying my dear sweet Paul. That's when I decided to call for our little meeting today."

She then looked at her family and took a sip of wine, a bite of bread and then some cheese. Gathering her thoughts she took one more sip raised her glass up and said "what a wonderful day that was as you all know we met at the Woodstock festival in 1969. How we met is certainly another story worth remembering but this one is of our wedding." She closed her eyes and wrapped her arms around her breast.

Jenny said "and what a wonderful story that is."

"Thank you, my best girlfriend ever. Now Paul set it all up and we were married by the lake in Montgomery, Alabama just like his parents were. It was a beautiful spring day and being outside by the lake made me think of when he first told me he loved me. We were by the Peachtree Creek, in Atlanta this was one of the stops on our way home from Woodstock." She took a breath and then said "Jenny you are next, I'm getting too passionate thinking about that day."

"Sure dear, I wish I was there for your special day, you were so beautiful in that dress. Your dad in those pictures looked very proud as he gave you away." She stopped and just smiled looking at her friend and then said "as you know Cory and I were married on your farm and you and Paul were the best hosts anyone could have asked for. He was Cory's best man and you were my maid of honor. Tamla you and Shasha were so cute in your pink dresses just throwing those rose pedals around."

Margo saw the tears of joy stream down Jenny's face and she said "that was an amazing day, you were so beautifully radiant in that light yellow dress and Cory was so handsome, dressed in a light blue suit. It was an honor to play our part, with such a fantastic couple and the truest of friends."

Jenny then said "that farm in Alabama was sure a special place for us all."

Shasha looked at Tamla and said "we should both tell our own version of that special day. So you go first and I'll follow after you like I've done joyfully all these blessed years."

She grabbed her by the face and kissed her like the day they were married and then said "I love you so much Shasha Greene!" Tamla was too chocked up to start right now so she took a sip or two of wine. At least more than one sip!

Brenda was so excited that she went over and got in between Tamla and Shasha and hugged them both.

Tamla gathered herself and said "we wanted our own tradition. Since our home was in Georgetown and near the Capital we decided on that area. Being in the Congress did have some perks, and the area did have some lovely parks. The one we picked was near the Potomac River and this spring day was very perfect. Not sunny but cloudy, the rain held off until that evening, it was so cool and pleasant. We both picked identical spring dresses, to show that two good friends in love are committing to spend their lives together."

Jenny then said "you both looked very lovely in your spring dresses, I couldn't have been even more happy."

Holding Jenny's hand Margo said "so true Jenny, so true indeed."

Acting like a little girl Shasha said "my turn, my turn!"

They all laughed and she pretended to pout until Jenny came over there and said "okay my little girl you can go next."

"Okay I like everything that was said so far only to add this. Having our moms and dads there with us was so very special and thank you Supreme Court for confirming our legal right to marriage."

Brenda looked at all the special women in her lives, then noticed behind the gazebo in the distance was Terames, and Coretta. She waved at them and said "you both will be at my wedding!" and then she looked at the others and said "your stories are all so very inspiring that I just hope my wedding is as wonderful."

Coming closer Terames said "that and more so, your wedding will be a very special day on Millennia for us all."

The family all knew this day would come and what a day it was. A large number of the inhabitants of Millennia were there to witness this special occasion of the first wedding ever on their planet. The ceremony would be outside and the reception will be in the Assembly.

Brad was there with his family and friends they were all as anxious as he was to get this started. The Miller's and the Greene's couldn't believe how spectacular everything was. Paul had driven the Fleetline that Cory made for him. The dragons were flying around in a perfect formation. One group would spray fire while the other iced it! Doing this in the distance made for a brilliantly bright light and then when the ice would put it out, it created beautiful billows of white steam.

Water was all around and the dolphins would swim in and out in sequence, in groups of six. They would jump up from the water, split up in different directions, then fall down below the water, and dive into another pool. Charley the whale would splash with a couple of his friends just to create a cymbal effect! Looking on, Shasha said to Tamla "look there's Blue Fin!"

The wedding platform was mixed with many different flowers. With plants that formed almost into a perfect rainbow. In the back were these two very large sea shells that stood up and below each one was a pearl the size of a basketball. The expense of this was nothing because all pitched in and helped to shape this big event. Brenda was a very special Elven person to all.

A huge bluish white cloud descended down from the heavens, it stopped and hung in the sky. Then everyone there watched as the dragons stopped their flying and the dolphins their jumping. A strong cool breeze swept through all below so powerful you could almost see it. A large ball of pure energy ascended up from the cloud, then a spark of light broke out, and CRACK lighting burst out of it from all sides!

Seconds later three dragons appeared dressed in royal apparel. One was black with a white stone and a crown. Another was white with a crown and a black stone. The third was different in that she had a tiara, a scepter in her hand, and she had no legs but, a powerful tail. On her back rode Terames the High Councilor of the Pleiades. Most knew who they all were but one wrote this as the description of their entrance.

"Welcome Coretta, Terames, and others to Brenda and Brad's wedding ceremony" Margo said as the ambassador of Millennia.

Coretta said "thank you Margo, this is a very special day because many will be married before going on their journey back to Earth."

Then floating down to the ground Terames said "let's get this party started."

Margo looked around and said "you heard her start the music."

Many creatures made noises and some Elven people played instruments. They all made the most beautiful music together. The birds sang, some dragons hummed, and dolphins squeaked, all in perfect harmony. This music was not traditional and the wedding did have a few upgrades but generally it was still a wedding.

The music stopped, the groom approached the platform with his men and the maids all stepped up and took their places. Tamla and Shasha walked down the aisle and sprinkled rose pedals. Then two organs from the distant mountains on each side played the wedding theme.

Brenda approached from one side and Paul from the other, she took his arm and they proceeded to walk down the aisle. She looked stunningly beautiful with her light brown complexion, dark black hair, and her big brown eyes that made you think of the deepest mahogany you ever seen. All covered and formed in her long white dress formed perfectly to shape her wonderful curves.

Her dress has a low cut in front with an opening in the back that formed a perfect oval shape. The lace was a very light blue with soft streaks of pink. Her hair was black with long curls that just barely moved but just enough to give them life as they flowed with her steps and the music.

Hearts pounding from Brad and Brenda you could just feel the vortex of love that emanated from them as they drew closer. Coming to a stop the minister asked "who gives the hand of this bride away."

Holding in his pride Paul said "I Paul Miller do."

Brenda stepped up next to Brad and Paul turned and walked to sit down next to Margo. Brad took her hand and smiled at her, she whispered "I love you."

The minister read their vows and asked "Brenda Greene-Miller do you take Brad Andrew Cole to be your husband?"

"Yes I do."

Then the minister asked "Brad Andrew Cole do you take Brenda Greene-Miller to be your wife?"

"Most assuredly I do."

"Please exchange rings and you are now married." They placed rings on each other's fingers "you may kiss and seal this marriage."

This kiss was so powerful that all in the crowd cheered and applauded for almost a minute. It seemed the kiss went that long too. Margo hugged Jenny, Jenny hugged Terames, Terames hugged Cory, Cory hugged Paul and smiled about it, Paul hugged Shasha, Shasha hugged Tamla and Tamla hugged Coretta.

The place settled down and all were quiet as Margo walked up to the platform. Some soft music played from the two organs and in the distance you could hear the birds sing a faint melodic sound. There she sang this;

True Love Delivers

Amazing this day, for here is the call
All shall witness this union of two
Where love for each other stands tall

Climb the hill, cross the rivers
Find inside yourself this fact
In all times, true love delivers!

Hear sounds of the world all around
Then she walks down the aisle
Creatures don't disturb her ground

Climb the hill, cross the rivers
Find inside yourself this fact
In all times, true love delivers!

Together as one they will be
Travelling through space and time
Onward to a distant galaxy

Climb the hill, cross the rivers
Find inside yourself this fact
In all times, true love delivers!

CHAPTER 2

Many more of Millennia's elven people were married and now need to learn how to live as a family like in the previous age. The current situation was very promising for the ones traveling to Earth. The Wayshowers and Indigos shared their stories from Earth and this seemed to benefit them greatly.

"Brad, I love being married to you" Brenda said as she awoke from their honeymoons. Since the planet Millennia has two moons they now changed honeymoon to plural.

He laid there with a big smile on his face and said "something I've wished for a long time my sweet angel."

Nestled in the green mountains this place they picked for their honeymoons was beautiful and near perfect. There was a waterfall coming down from one of the tall mountains flowing into a crystal clear river that could be seen from their balcony. With a full course breakfast waiting for them, they knew that these nutrients and proteins would come in handy today.

"This orange juice is delicious and I think we should take some of these nuts with us on our hike today" Brad said enjoying a chocolate and macadamia nut muffin.

Taking a sip of some mint tea Brenda said "good idea."

After an early morning interlude their food settled and they took off for an adventure. The plan was to walk up one of the smaller mountains and have lunch at this renowned restaurant on the top. Then walk back down, make a stop at the room and change clothes for some tennis. Brad played before on Earth and now since he couldn't fly he decided to try tennis again. She never played much tennis but preferred golf with her grandpa. Brad beat her but he was a little surprised at how well she could run down the shots and he didn't unleash his Andy Roddick serve on her because just like Paul and Cory, he too was a gentleman.

As they took the bus back home Brenda was surprised with who waited at the station to drive them to Paul and Margo's home. Getting off the bus Cory and Jenny were there to take them back home in this new vehicle Cory had built himself and this one was very amazing. All the while Jenny wanted to be with her granddaughter so they rode in the back. The men talked about farming and what type of equipment would be used on the new Earth.

Pulling into the drive Brenda was perplexed; she didn't remember Paul's Fleetline being yellow? She looked at Jenny and said "what happened to Paul's car? Why did he paint it?"

Cory and Jenny both smiled, then Jenny said "dear that's your new car."

"OMG" That was all she could say.

Brad being the optimist said "good we can use it to drive home later."

Brenda looked puzzled again and said "home, what home?"

"You'll see soon enough."

Going inside after they checked out the car, they were greeted by Margo and Paul, who, were waiting for Brad to tell her his surprise. First things first they had to tell all about their honeymoons and how wonderful it was. Brenda talked about the beautiful gardens and Brad told them how he liked the green clay tennis courts. But after a little snack and reflection they were all ready for what Brad had planned.

Brad ran out to their car and said "who wants to ride with us?"

Paul said "you two ride together and talk we'll double up and follow."

Cory said "Paul can I drive the Fleetline?"

"Sure buddy be my guest."

Driving down the winding road and past the hydro power plant, they took in the fresh country air and felt so alive today. Passing the forest of big tall trees and then a very large lake they were just intrigued with this beautiful planet. Brad turned right down a dirt road and Brenda looked at him and smiled. All she could think about was the farm in Alabama, this made her feel warm inside.

As the car went over the hill she could see the farm and all she said was "oh my dear, this is perfect!"

He just smiled and said "wait until you see inside."

They all parked. Then Margo, Paul, Jenny and Cory sat there all nostalgic about how it reminded them of the old farm. Brenda and Brad approached the car and after opening her door Jenny said to Brenda "why didn't you invite Tamla and Shasha?"

"I couldn't, I didn't know about this until now."

"True I forgot about that." Jenny then looked at Brad and said "Then Mr. Cole do you have an answer?"

He looked at them all and made a crazy face then threw his arms up and said "it was difficult enough to keep this secret from you four and Brenda."

They were all out and walking to the door and stopped and as they all laughed at his silly expressions.

Paul said "Mr. Cole you are an Italian using your hands to talk." He then put his arm around him and said "and we do love you."

The home was wonderfully small it only had two bedrooms, two full baths, and a very large study for Brenda. Brad was very quick to point out that his office was the big barn with the green roof outside. The farm also had over 50 acres. The purpose was to grow all types of food and store seeds for the trip to Earth. He did play a major role in current food production and preparing powdered food for the ships computer on their journey.

Soon they all walked around the farm after checking out the house. Brad treated them to a light lunch he had prepared, some fruits and vegetables from the farm.

Although the food was a little different than before it was still incredibly tasty. Conversations went from their honeymoons to the trip to Earth. Jenny asked the big questions "are you two planning to have children?" After she said this she quickly asked the rest "can they do that here?"

Paul spoke as they all looked stumped and said "I don't know if things have changed here to permit that." Putting his hand on his chin like he does when in deep thought, he completed it by saying "probably not now but maybe after they enter their new bodies."

Silence filled the room and Brenda asked Margo "can you see what Terames has to say about that?"

"I sure will dear, that would be very wonderful if that's what you two want."

Cory said "maybe they should wait until they are settled in on the new Earth? I mean it could be difficult setting up a new civilization."

Looking over at Cory, Brad said "I couldn't agree more." He then held Brenda's hand and said "I'm sure you all will visit us then, so you may see all the children Brenda plans to bless me with."

For a brief moment Brenda was angry, then blushed and finally looked at Brad and smiled. She said "okay Mr. Cole but I will make sure you do more than your fair share of raising them."

They all laughed and the vibrations were so very high that all hugged and remembered the joys of raising their own children. Paul picked up the keys and said "come on seniors let's go and leave these young love birds to enjoy their first night on the farm."

The party on the farm was big, Tamla and Shasha were there and so happy for their sweet girl. Brenda always made them proud and this was just another one of those times.

It seemed after the celebration and the festivities the people broke off into two major groups; one was the farmers and engineers, the second were the doctors and politicians, while the wizards joined both groups. Group one left the house and went to the barn and then the fields to inspect the crops. Group two just went outside by the lake and formed into a circle around the gazebo.

Cory and Paul were with some of the engineers over by one of the big barns looking at the equipment. You would be surprised at how familiar this equipment was from Earth's time of organic farming. Brad would think back to how wonderful life was when people bought locally and knew the farmers as friends and neighbors. Now he had his chance to bring this period back and learn from the mistakes that had led to greed coming in to destroy that harmonious society. He walked over to them and asked "do you two have questions?"

Cory said "yes I do, how do you like the equipment we made and designed for you?"

Paul chuckled and said "Cory you are a very cognizant engineer. Always following your creations and making sure they are performing to their specifications."

Brad slapped Paul on the back and said "Mr. Wizard it sounds like you know plenty about this too." He smiled at Cory and said "they are working perfectly for now. However as I use them I will take notes and let you know of any improvements."

They all left the equipment and then joined the rest of them by the fields. Many of them were already studying and taking samples from the crops and soil. Brad and the others were careful not to interrupt them while they were gathering their materials for scientific study later.

Before this the wizards did a lot of study to determine the differences from Earth's soil. They did find some useful differences and one of their projects was to bring them to Earth and meld them into the soil. This has been completed in the lab and now Brad will test this in his fields.

"Very impressive Brad" Paul said and then he noticed some deer gleaning in another field of corn. He turned back to

Brad and asked "have you found that letting the dear graze to be beneficial?"

"Yes, I think it is, and I plan on leaving a couple of fields open during harvest. The deer not only will gain nourishment and leave their excretion, but I will turn those fields over in the spring and let them sit a full year. My calculations show that this will create a very fertile soil and replenish the land."

"Wow very impressive Brad! Now I see why you are so missed at the castle."

"Thank you Paul, your guidance has helped me in my new endeavor." He then looked at Cory and said "and I do like the way this equipment feels like a part me."

That made Cory feel good and Paul couldn't be happier with him. They both knew that he would be more than capable of helping his fellow travelers when they are back on Earth.

Brenda was talking with Shasha and noticed a cloud in the sky. This was a dark cloud that had been noticed before so you would think she and the rest wouldn't be afraid but... She moved closer to Shasha and said "hold me, I'm scared."

Traveling back in time Shasha said "oh my sweet baby girl, don't be afraid we know that it is Terames the High Councilor." She then put her arms around her and hugged her."

Feeling that something important was about to happen. Margo said to the group "all prepare to receive the High Councilor."

Even the air seemed to go quiet and then the lighting flashed, a sonic boom followed. The cloud broke, then dissolved, and once again there appeared three beautiful dragons with Terames riding on the back of one of them.

What a way to start a political meeting and to know that the people invited to this party were a select group of close advisors and fellow Wayshowers. Terames flew off of Coretta then descended down and landed in the middle of the gazebo. All were in a circle around and waited to hear her words. Margo then said "welcome Your Grace we are honored to have you join us."

"Thank you Margo, please join me up here with Tamla and Brenda also."

There they were, Coretta had changed back into Ambrosia, and Terames stood next to her. To Terames' left, was Margo, then Tamla and last was Brenda, who stood next to her in that order. It was so poetic that the lineage was there in chronological order.

Ambrosia was then ready to speak. The lighting and thunder alerted the farmers, engineers, and the wizards. Once they arrived, settled down, she began to talk, and this is what she said.

"My people as you probably already know this group of ladies here are part of my lineage. They will all become the High Councilor one day. What this means is we need to strengthen our connections of love and loyalty because we will all be tested at different levels soon. If it hasn't been said yet, you should know this; that these one thousand years are an opportunity to rest and to grow in ascension. With that said I want you all to know that these ladies are here to lead to and love you all. Together we are strong against all forces that can weaken and destroy our resolve. Please support them and know that they each will have access to one another to resolve all situations that may arise."

She then stepped back and all acknowledged her with "we love you Ambrosia."

The girls up there, all spoke in order after her, and then shared what was on their hearts. When the day was over Margo and Paul went home and just enjoyed each other's company. That morning when the sun arose and the two moons were still visible Margo wrote the most beautiful song.

Our Lineage

We are one, so that we will always be sure.
Together helping one another our mission is.
The love that flows from each heart is pure.

Holding, touching, and feeling, love to surround.
Seeing, believing, teaching, and helping all around.

Living in our lineage we do this first.
Stronger than steel, yes our Spirits are.
Crossing the river we quench our thirst.

Holding, touching, and feeling, love to surround.
Seeing, believing, teaching, and helping all around.

Going back in time we take life in our own hands.
Learning and becoming all we will ascend.
Life after life, we are the hour glass, full of sand.

Holding, touching, and feeling, love to surround.
Seeing, believing, teaching, and helping all around.

This is our lineage of love.

He noticed that she was gone and when he left the room he could feel a presence of something in the air. After grabbing a cup of fresh brewed tea, he then slipped on his sandals. Opening the back door and looking out at the lake he could see a light in the gazebo. Walking closer he then heard her sing this new song, and not wanting to disturb her, he just sat on the ground and enjoyed listening to his love sing. The lyrics were beautiful but when she sang the chorus he was taken in and shed a happy tear.

The Sun was slowly making its way up over the lake. Paul stood up and approached her. She was filled with the Spirit of Light and radiated competing only with the Sun. He could only watch and wait for the Source to be finished with her. She then noticed him and looking at him like an abandoned puppy she said "I need you."

Wasting no time he moved to her quickly and safely. Wrapping his arms around her then looking into her eyes he kissed her above her eyes. Right in the middle of her forehead, she responded by squeezing him tight and finding his lips and planting all her feelings in this kiss.

CHAPTER 3

The night was growing old and she still hadn't told him how she felt. He was always quiet and she being in politics could not say enough. Tonight would be different. She had talked with him about getting married before and he was all for it. Dory just couldn't wait for him to ask the question, so she planned this evening to ask him.

Okay that's not the way it's supposed to happen, right? Well this is a different world and some of the customs from the old Earth didn't all translate back here again. One custom that was established early on was that there were to be no masculine or feminine standards.

The waiter was walking over to tell them that the café' would be closing soon. She spotted him and then made up her mind that as soon as the waiter left she was going to pop the question. Dory told him that they would be leaving soon. The waiter acknowledged her and then turned and headed for the kitchen. Reaching in her pocket for the ring, she pulled out the box and handed it to Rich and then said "here ask me to marry you and then give me this ring!"

He said with a lump in his throat "yes my sweet, I will do that." He slid over from his chair and got down on one knee and then opening the box he said "Dory will you marry me?"

Even though she set the whole thing up, she still cried happy tears and said "yes I will gladly marry you Rich."

They were then asked to leave, because the café' was now closed. They left a sizable tip and then gladly left and walked the street holding hands and talking about their wedding. Rich and Dory would be just one of many couples to be married in the next several years.

Coretta and Terames were very pleased with how the progress of Millennia was going. Couples were getting married, discoveries were being made and the ships were being built. There were a lot of things told to Margo and some to the rest also, but there still were some secrets kept, and they will stay that way until the time is right.

Coretta said "Things are going just as planned, don't you think?"

"Yes they are and I wonder what changes will happen to us next?"

"Well Terames, I'm sure you will become a dragon and I have no idea what's in store for me." Looking down on Millennia she said "you know Margo is on her way back up here and eventually she will return our people to another level of greatness as she did before."

"Yes, and you did a fine job as Ambrosia."

"Thank you dear, it's amazing that your time is almost up too."

They reminisced for a while longer and then returned home.

The streets were starting to get busy with the new cars that Cory helped make. Everyone was working, and enjoyed feeling important by doing what their hearts desired. There was one thing the people made sure they did together and that was collaborate. The plans are being made for Tamla to succeed Margo as the planet's High Councilor.

Arriving at the Assembly Shasha was parking the van the girls used to car-pool in. The ride was filled with talk about Brenda's wedding and how beautiful it was. She was so excited after her honeymoons that she wasn't sure politics would receive her best right now. Although gratitude and peace were on her mind she couldn't get Brad out of her thoughts. With her arm around her Jenny said "he is such a wonderful man, and we all believe that will translate into him being a great husband."

"Thanks I'm sure you both are correct."

Margo nodded her head yes and said "okay enough talk about weddings, husbands and honeymoons." With her arms opened wide she said "okay my girls let's start off our workday at the Assembly with a round of hugs."

One after another they gave her a hug and then proceeded into the Assembly building. Today's business was light and Margo would start teaching Tamla to be the next High Councilor. Jenny was teaching Shasha the things she would need to know to support Tamla and to assume the High Councilor position if needed. Now they had all spent more than a lifetime together but this teaching still needed to happen. While in the group Brenda and James would shadow their new positions on Earth and also learn more about each other too.

During one of their breaks Brenda and James were full of questions that were hard to answer, if answered at all. One of the first was asked by James to Jenny and Shasha when he said "are we going to take the current constitution with us and if we do will it reference Millennia?"

Jenny answered him and said "no it will reference the planets that you are to have come from?"

Looking puzzled Brenda said "why are we going to lose our memories?"

Margo said "because if you could remember all of your history, you wouldn't have much of a sense of discovery, would you?"

They all smiled and Jenny said "that's why I love you so much Margo your diplomacy in explaining things is unequalled."

"Why thank you my dear friend."

The days seemed to be getting longer for most people on Millennia and just Paul happened to be one of them. After a day at the castle studying the new bodies on the computer, he ran several scenarios of possible problems to come on Earth, and began to become sad, very sad. This was a feeling he hadn't felt in a long time and he wasn't sure what this meant.

Yes he did own a beautiful 46 Fleetline car and he could drive it to work at the castle. This was something that just didn't feel right to him unless he was going to use it for a carpool so instead he took the bus there every day. On his ride home he meditated on these thoughts that made him sad. By the time he cleared his mind he was almost home, then his thoughts turned to Margo, and to spending time with her.

Stepping off the bus and walking down the street he was captivated with planning their evening. He thought of an elegant dinner with wine, spending some time in the hot tub, and after that some love making. Walking in the door to find she wasn't there, this made him sad until he heard her in the kitchen. "There you are" he said walking down the passageway. He walked up behind her at the sink and put his arms around her.

"Well hello to you to dear" she said and then turned around to kiss him.

"This is what I needed all day, I missed you today more than ever for some reason."

"I think with the changes that are coming soon we are all anxious."

While helping her prepare dinner, he reflected on his sadness of the day. Caught up in the dilemma not to talk about it, and ruin the evening. His hope is that he can suppress it, and not wreak his plans for the night. He was doing fine suppressing them until she asked "what's the matter you look sad?"

"I'm not sure I've felt this way all day. I didn't want to mention it tonight and ruin our evening."

"Don't be silly, if something bothers you, then it damn well bothers me."

"There you go again helping me solve my problems."

She laughed and grabbed his face, kissed him and then said "our problems, dear."

He kissed her back and said "Okay here goes, I think this new Earth project we are working on has me thinking about how we have lived all these years here in almost perfection. I was doing some work on some scenarios of problems of this Earth project then I felt like I had a premonition of sadness and pain to come. A cold chill came over me and I was sad all day."

Looking at him she could then feel the sadness and she said to him "I will ask mom and Coretta about this." She then thought maybe I'll take the girls with me to help understand it. "Is there more you can tell me about this premonition of pain?"

"Well I'm not sure if we have been told all about Earth from the higher ups or if this will happen in the future there. One thing I feel is that they should at least prepare for the unexpected." He then looked at her and noticed she was crying. "Are you sensing something?"

"Yes, I am, and I agree they need to be prepared for any contingency." Then she wrote their thoughts down on her tablet and said "okay we will deal with this tomorrow. Tonight is ours for fun and pleasure. So let's have some more wine!"

This was a special evening and yes they did forget about the sadness. For one thing they learned that being happy created a bridge in their Spirits to overcome any obstacle. The French say it best *Une soirée pleine d'amour* and *an evening full of love* it was.

The next day they both went to work planning and searching for information about their feelings of the Earth mission and the possibility of trouble. He went to pick Cory up, drive out to Brad's farm, and then to discuss their plans to prepare for this. Margo contacted Jenny and their chain began. She contacted Shasha and Tamla then they contacted Brenda.

After he picked Cory up Jenny headed over to Margo's place. Driving to the farm Paul and Cory came up with several plans. These two and Brad will work out some ideas for their group, named the Rebels to help them carry out the plans of the Pleiades. A day on the farm and fresh air helped these three power brokers to come up with at least three strong plans. Paul was very pleased with their ideas and said "gentlemen we now should gather the rest of the Rebels and finalize this."

Brad said "that's an excellent idea."

Cory seconded the motion and off they went bringing Brad along with them.

The girls summoned Coretta and Terames to visit and discuss this. Although these girls aren't planners they do like to talk about how to deal with problems or possible ones diplomatically. Terames replied back and said "meet us in the gazebo and bring some sweet white wine. We will bring you some future information to plan for."

Before this meeting began Margo said to Tamla "dear I want you to take the lead in this and Shasha you will support her."

"Huh, mom do you think I'm ready?" She said looking flabbergasted.

"Yes, you've been ready for a long time."

In this meeting they were given some future Earth information. It was then decided by Tamla that something will be written in their new Constitution to guide them diplomatically through these types of emergencies. The wine was drunk and they all laughed and enjoyed each other's company.

The two groups got together that evening and made plans to gather their fellow Rebels and they did just that. The security equipment was designed and the emergency plans added to the Earth's Constitution. There will be more premonitions to deal with until the launch day.

We are now at the Cole farm with Brenda and Brad. Trouble in paradise, could it be? Well this just might be a sign of things to come, but let's not speculate too much. There are some big changes coming and it's time to work through the uncertainty of life back in the third dimension.

Brenda arrives home from a day at the Assembly working with Margo, Jenny, Tamla, Shasha and James on the new song for the new Earth's Constitution. Very tired but still inspired with what they decided on and later Margo will put it all into a song.

Brad sees her walking up the walkway and there his heart opens up to her. Opening the door and rushing to her he grabs her briefcase and puts his arms around her waist. Their eyes meet and he kisses her forehead right between her eyes and says "I love you my precious girl."

"You are so good to me, I love you too."

With a chuckle and a Han Solo look he said "I know."

Inside the home she plops on the couch and going with this train of thought she says "what's for dinner?"

"The chef has a marvelous dinner planned, so you sit there and wait for me to summon you to the dining room table."

He so enjoyed cooking especially since it all can from his farm. On the farm he had some workers during the day because this was also a training center for the Earth journey. Dinner was great and she so enjoyed being taken care of and the wine was made from the grapes grown on their farm. It seems these two went from a lifetime on Earth before as medical doctors specializing in the heart and nerves to being a politician and a farmer. Whatever they would do they will be successful at it.

With the next day off and breakfast eaten they decided to discuss the current plans they had worked on during the last couple of days. "Okay dear tell me about this new song Margo is working on for our Constitution?"

"It's going to be great, we all took the information from our conference with the Rebels and then worked it out yesterday." Then she stretched her arms, yawned and said "here goes. If we run into a hostile entity, human, animal or other we will first gather all the information we can on them. This will be used to ascertain how we can communicate a peace treaty with them. After we do, we will have a devise to translate all forms of known language." Taking a break she stood up and then sat back down. This was also her way of giving him time to process the information she gave him.

Acknowledging what she was doing he acted like a robot and then said "okay information received, now proceed please."

"You're funny, ha. After communicating with the threat, we will then send out music designed to calm their aggression, or at the least prepare them for some diplomatic negotiations." Folding her arms she said "What do you think?"

He followed the rule of listening to what someone had to say and to try your best to let those words create an image. Then processing what she said he had to ask her this "It all sounds good so what are the plans for when diplomacy doesn't work?"

For a few minutes they were both quiet. Brad was doing his best job to not say anything until after she responded. So when she did, this is what she said "I see your point and I believe that we politicians just feel that we can solve all problems without force. Now let me hear what you men came up with?"

"Well, we don't feel that this is the desired method but here goes. If our settlement were to be attacked or threatened by a hostile force, then this is how we would handle it. A security force would have been created to police our settlement and protect us from any outside aggression too." Making a slightly confused face he then looked at her and smiled.

Not thinking about what she said, the words "that's stupid!" just blurted out. He didn't even wait to hear her apologize.

"Thanks!" he said very loudly and then got up and went outside to the barn. There he worked very hard to grow food and learn better methods to take care of the land and animals. What she said really hurt him, to be told by the one he loved so much that the plan he had a part in the making was stupid.

Normally she would have just followed him, but this time she felt that he didn't need to leave. Although what she said was wrong, or at the least didn't show any tact. With tears she was very sad at what she said, but she felt she couldn't give in to him right now. They both spent the evening and the next day apart from each other.

Without a word to anyone about their argument both Brenda and Brad spent the day as if nothing had happened. He could jump on a tractor and spend his day plowing a field and being alone, she however was in the Assembly with all her fellow politicians.

"Brenda is there something wrong?" Tamla asked worried about her little girl.

Stepplng up to the platform to see what was going on Shasha looked at her lover and their daughter then she also asked "is there something wrong?"

Tamla grabbed her by the hand and then took Brenda's and said "let's go to our office and talk about this."

Tamla grabbed three tea cups and then filled them with some spiced tea and said "here girls now let's talk." She then sat down in one of the guest chairs and looked at Brenda and said "okay little girl, what's wrong?"

"I said something I shouldn't have to Brad the other night and now he's mad at me."

"Did you apologize to him?"

"No, he left and slept in the barn and I haven't seen him since he left."

Shasha then said "well what exactly did you say?"

"Well were talking about the new song about protection from a hostile force. I told him our plan first and then he told me the plan that he, Paul and Cory came up with and I said it was stupid."

The room was quiet very quiet, Shasha and Tamla looked at each other with their eyes wide open. Brenda looked at them both and said "what?"

Tamla held her hand and said "dear why did you say that to him?"

"I didn't mean to it just slipped out."

Shasha asked her "what was so stupid?"

"They were talking about having a police security force full time. So when there were threats foreign or domestic the force can protect us. He didn't seem to think that diplomacy would always work."

Both Shasha and Tamla gave her some good advice and they understood that times are changing and this was part of her test for leadership. She wanted to take some time to let this blow over so with a text message to Brad she told him she needed to spend time with her parents and that she was sorry for what she said.

In the cool of the evening after dinner with her parents she felt like a little girl again. He wasn't angry just hurt and even though she said the plan was stupid by his leaving he gave her no time to explain or apologize. Now he would miss her and hopefully when she returned home they could correct this.

A few days went by where Brenda and Brad discussed the two plans together. At the Assembly Margo held off on writing her song for the plan she and the other politicians worked out. Since Tamla was taking the lead in this she put the song on hold until they first studied the plan from Paul and Cory. Today they would visit the Assembly and work with Margo's people to finalize this.

"Paul I like the plan for a security force that protects from any threats domestic or foreign" Tamla said as she began the discussion.

"Thanks, we like your plan with the music being sent out as an early attempt to calm the threat." He said and then opened his arms and said "we certainly welcome resolving them peacefully."

Brenda and Brad decided to just sit and watch the others work this all out. They both had a Spirit to observe life on Millennia knowing that their home will soon be back on Earth.

Cory processed what was being said, he then went on to say "I like where this is going. The plan is being consciously conceived to be derived with love and trust of each side."

Jenny smiled and said "there goes my man using those big words to bring a certain understanding to this that can't be argued with."

Later that evening Margo wrote this song to reflect the feelings of their meeting.

Protection by Faith

Hostile forces on the move, they are coming today.
Who can stop them, do we have this power?
Soothing the heart with vibrations will be one way.

Hoping doesn't prevent trouble.
Only Faith will protect like a bubble.

A force made of weapons that will stun and not kill.
Using our hearts we guide our minds this way.
Not shooting our supposed enemy just for a thrill.

Hoping doesn't prevent trouble.
Only Faith will protect like a bubble.

This force is used for peace and not for war.
Volunteers rotate through to include all.
We bring hope, love, and faith to our shore.

Hoping doesn't prevent trouble.
Only Faith will protect like a bubble.

CHAPTER 4

Time passes and now the ships are ready for the journey. Margo assembles her people to begin the countdown and for them to prepare to inhabit their new bodies. To them this could not have come any sooner since they have been working hard to accomplish this.

The people traveling to Earth have been going through many new emotional changes. Once the third dimension came back to include gravity it was a welcomed change at first. All were very positive to experience pain and pleasure again. Many were married. Some went to school to learn a new profession, they now desired. Brenda and Brad learned what it was like to disagree and even split up for a time. They weren't alone, many people had different opinions and there was some apparent strife.

After a couple of weeks of intense work, Paul was working with Cory, and he asked him "what do you think, do you think we prepared them good enough for the journey?"

"Well, let's hope so. Maybe your premonition was given to you to make sure they are."

"I just wish we could go with them." He then looked at the ships and gave some workers directions on loading. Cory smiled at him and then Paul said "you sure have been a great help all these centuries my friend."

"I can't believe how much time has gone by. Now their new bodies are ready too."

This day finally came to an end and the night would be full of surprises. Dreamland was the plan from the heavens tonight. There they would either travel to their Pleiadian star or if in the Assembly they went to the High Council. Margo was there with Paul just like the first time in 1969 at the Woodstock concert were she held his hand and said "I'm a little nervous about what's going to happen."

"You will be fine I have the utmost confidence in you." He then brought her hand to his lips and kissed it just like the southern gentleman he is.

"Thank you dear you are the wind beneath my wings"

He smiled and said "as long as my hot air will help you fly, you will always have it."

Terames walked up and said "come on my children, we have things to attend." Once she had them walking toward the Council she went to locate Tamla and Brenda.

They seemed to just take their own sweet time getting in their seats. Terames was anxious and walked around getting them ready just like herding cattle. Once the High Council was ready she hurried to the back of the podium to prepare for her announcement.

The gavel struck hard and Leto said "all rise for the High Councilor Terames."

Walking up to the podium Terames said "welcome all members and guests. We are so glad we could kidnap you in your dreams and bring you here tonight." She shook her head and smiled.

She proceeded to explain to them that this night three things will happen. The original Wayshowers would leave there bodies and translate their eternal Light beings back to the Pleiades. The next group who are normally called the Indigo's will stay on Millennia and go back to the fifth dimension. Finally the last souls to translate to Millennia from Earth will enter new bodies tonight and travel back to the new earth.

Then the lights went dim and she stepped away from the podium where Leto took her place and she went in the back and returned with a box. Leto looked back at her and then turned to face the Assembly and said "would Millennia's High Councilor Margo please approach the front?"

As Margo walked towards the front Terames stepped down with the box and stood in front of the podium and waited for her. Looking at her daughter she smiled and when Margo approached her Terames said in a low voice "I am so proud of you."

Margo softly relied "Thanks mom, I love you."

Leto made the announcement that Margo is now to become the new High Councilor of the Pleiades. Terames presented her with her new outfit to acknowledge her title. When she was done she then told Margo to go into the back room and change.

The Assembly took a fifteen minute break until Margo returned as the new High Councilor and with a box of her own.

This time she stood in front of the podium and Leto called Tamla to present herself to the new High Councilor. Margo whispered to her "you are so very special and I love you."

Leaning toward Margo she gave her a big hug and the whole Assembly made an "awe" sound.

Another announcement was made by Leto, this time it was to declare the new High Councilor of the planet Millennia. Her name is Tamla, daughter of Margo and Paul Miller.

Tamla took her new outfit and left to change in the back room. Margo waited for her and noticed that Terames was missing. She said to Leto "where has Terames gone?"

He just smiled at her and said "she will return."

Just then Tamla returned and hugged Margo then both bowed to the Assembly as they received applause. The Assembly got quiet very quickly and looked amazed. Margo and Tamla turned to see behind them and there stood the most beautiful white dragon with black trim and a purple stone on her chest. Margo said "Your Grace Terames, is that you?"

"Yes it is dear daughter and my new name is Jillela."

"Well that's going to take some getting used to."

Jillela chuckled and Margo said "what's so funny?"

"Well dear, your new name is Daanic."

Tamla maintained her name and she asked Jillela why she didn't have a new one. She was told that is because she's not changing into a new form of being, yet.

No one left this dream after the leadership shifted their roles up. In fact what happened next is what they all have been working on for many years. Paul located Cory and said "well my friend, are we ready to load up the ships?"

"You know it, let's start assigning them to their ships and assign them their duties."

The strange thing that was happening was that this was a dream and the one hundred and forty-four thousand Wayshowers thought that they were going to help load the ships. Instead they left their bodies during this dream. As was said before, the body didn't die it just vanished back into the ether all around where they slept. The Indigo's took over and helped the Earth's new Wayshowers on their journey.

Tamla took charge, she and Shasha were a team to be proud of, and that's exactly what Jillela and Daanic were.

"Brenda I think you know that you are now the leader of the new Earthlings." Tamla said to her.

"Yes I do mom and I need to go locate James to start loading into our new bodies. I'm not really sure how we are to do this"

Brenda found James and they gathered all two hundred million for the transition. They were all in the predetermined places for this. While they were there talking and sharing their old stories from Earth a great sleep came over them. Shasha noticed what was happening and she took hold of Tamla's hand and said "this is so amazing."

"Yes it is and they are all so brave. I will miss them."

"Yes my love we will all miss them."

That morning when the two moons went away and the sun rose up Millennia was different. There were many people gone and it had returned to the fourth dimension again. From the Pleiades the new High Councilor Daanic participated in some and observed the rest of the events of this powerful dream.

Galactic Changes

Where do I begin with this story of galactic changes?
Maybe I'll just breathe and collect all my thoughts.
I'll start with the leadership promotion of these Sages.

Galactic changes are now here.
Galactic changes without fear.

One moved up from her post as the High Councilor.
She then transformed into a dragon so she could fly.
This was accomplished because all believed in her.

Galactic changes are for one and all.
Galactic changes for big and small.

Her daughter would now guide the seven stars above.
A new name is given for her Spirit without a form.
This a beautiful sight to witness this woman full of love.

Galactic changes are now sounding.
Galactic changes with love abounding.

The third one is promoted with blessings and will now lead.
She is full of knowledge, fairness, compassion and kindness.
A royal she is for in this line a daughter of the galactic seed.

Galactic changes bring peace and hope.
Galactic changes by using faith to rope.
Galactic changes in our universe.

The ships are gone and the Wayshowers are back on the Pleiades. They all have new names and look different, but they have retained all their memories. Being so closely connected to the Energy source of the Universe their thought capacity is enormous. With that said we won't really hear from them for a while except the High Councilor Daanic and Jenny when they help Tamla and Shasha on Millennia.

Deep in space they awake in their new bodies, with no correct memories of who they really are. Their memories have been cleared and new ones given to them that aren't exactly true but they will assist in the new plan. The High Council didn't see any need to change their names since their memories of them are gone.

Brenda awakes sitting in the Captain's seat, she knows that she is their leader and James is second in command. She asks him "Commander give your report on our current location."

"Aye Captain, we are currently travelling through this present galaxy which is 50 million light years from Earth."

"What's our current speed?"

"Warp 8, Captain."

"Meet me in the Captain's conference room in fifteen minutes."

"Aye, Captain."

She left the bridge and Commander James met her shortly thereafter. As he entered the room, she wasn't sure how to talk with him about what was on her mind, and she said "James would you like some coffee?"

"Sure but no sugar just cream."

"Okay, I'm sure you don't know why I asked for you here." Doing her best to say these words, she contemplated how to ask him, finally she broke the silence, and said "do you feel like you just woke up from a dream and now you are here on this ship travelling through the galaxy?"

Knowing he could trust her, he was still trying to be careful and said "I'm not sure if I feel all that, but something is strange."

"That's good enough for me at least I'm not crazy."

"Captain I think we know differently and that we are crazy. I mean we left our home to travel across the galaxy to find this planet called Earth. One that we have never been to before and only through stories have we heard of it."

"Commander you and I certainly have our work cut for each us. I suggest we stick together like glue and keep this very large crew on this path."

"Aye, Captain!"

"Thanks James that will be all. Please return to the bridge and take the helm. I need to think through some things and chart our plan."

Brenda was reminiscing about her time on her planet of Fyrooth. There she lived on a farm and her mom was a doctor and dad worked in government. Their life was so simple, prosperous, and all three planets traded with each other. At least until some business tycoons had a disagreement.

It was terrible since the older generation were very nationalistic and itching for war. The propaganda was almost laughable to the younger people. They couldn't understand how the elders could believe such garbage. So because the younger people on all three planets could see through this malaise, they refused to take up arms.

All three peoples tried to work this out diplomatically but the propaganda they believed was so strong that they wouldn't trust each other. Some foods that the people of Fyrooth depended on from Tyreega were cut-off. Then in turn Fyrooth cancelled medical supplies that Tyreega needed. Hydrumn tried to take advantage of this and supply each side with armaments for war.

During a diplomatic negotiation some secret talks of the ambassadors of Hydrumn were intercepted by Tyreega. Instead of using this information to side against Fyrooth, Tyreega chose not to trust Hydrumn because of their plans.

For the first several years the planets would lob missiles at each other. Mostly the missiles were sent to small towns and scarcely populated areas. Until the people became tired of the war machine that had been created, taxes were leveled to support the production of missiles, and many hours and materials to build them.

Politicians of Hydrumn feared the people would revolt at the ballot box. All three branches voted to conscript the young to launch an attack on Fyrooth. Intelligence conferred the possibility of conquering them and then using their missiles to cause Tyreega to surrender. Satellites by Tyreega confirmed a large military build-up on Hydrumn and this could only mean an attack. Knowing that no matter which one they attacked it would not benefit the other so Tyreega shared this intelligence with Fyrooth.

Hydrumn's plan was foiled and the other planets conscripted their young to prepare for war. Being conscious of what was going on a large number of the young people on all three planets were in communications all along. They used a secret code to plan their escape from their waring planets. It took a few years and some lives to achieve this but here they are some two hundred million travelling through space in search of a planet called Earth.

CHAPTER 5

The days of visiting Ambrosia on the High Council were over. Daanic (Margo) remembered when her mom was not even an Elder, this was when she, and Ringo reported to their chief. Thinking back on all this was a lot to process and right now her heart was very heavy with concerns of Brenda and her people. Coretta (Ambrosia) was the High Councilor then until Daanic's mom took over and now she is.

She visited the council many times with her family from her star called Maia. With her now living there for however long will take some getting used to. At first they weren't sure if adjusting to this new form would be acceptable. Sure life is different outside of a physical form, when you've lived so many lives on Earth, and can now recall them all with clarity.

On this plane of existence time has no bearing whatsoever. Whenever Daanic wanted to communicate with Paul all that was needed was to think about him. A dream is something that can leave a lasting memory and it's an opportunity for your soul to travel to exotic places. What the Wayshowers are now experiencing again on this plane is even more powerful. Here they simply recall a memory and presto they are living it all over again.

A dragon is what her mom Terames had become and what a beautiful one she is. In the last dream when she was promoted Daanic looked for Coretta and didn't see her. After Terames arrived, who now has become a dragon named Jillela, Daanic noticed a magnificent Alicorn, and she just wondered who it was. This was something to ask Jillela the next time she would visit her in a dream.

Why would they not worry about their daughter, after all they are our girls aren't they? That was a rhetorical question if ever there was one.

Shasha felt as worried as Tamla and she had a plan to deal with this. Looking at her friend she said "dear let's go on an official trip into the Milky Way galaxy shall we?"

Shaking her head and then rubbing her chin, Tamla was trying her best to look like *The Thinking Man* except being a female elven and certainly not nude. She responded with "is that a rhetorical question?"

Shasha laughed so loud that Tamla said "whoa, keep it down or everyone will want in on our trip."

"The more the merrier right, so what's your plan?"

Tamla looked puzzled and said "I thought you had a plan?"

After sitting there and sipping their tea for a while, the plan was not formalizing itself. So they both agreed to just meditate and wait for their energies to tap into the universe and receive their mission.

It didn't take more than thirty minutes of an Earthly time before Shasha spoke. She opened her eyes and said "eureka, I've got it! We will go on a mission to Earth to obtain information of the new formed planet."

Patiently listening to her Tamla asked "so when do we see our little girl Brenda?"

Smiling and shaking her head, Shasha kissed Tamla smack on the lips, and then said "during the trip to Earth. We will visit her in our dreams silly."

Now the plan will be formulated from the information that they both received from the Universe during their meditation. They both learned from their mothers how to just get quiet and let their inner self connect to the Universal Source inside.

With James gone, Lemuria and Atlantis are now both governed by the Assembly. The government has kept most of their laws from when Margo was the High Councilor. Tamla is the High Councilor and Shasha is her second in command who travels to Lemuria often to meet with their leaders. Even though they are the leaders it is a democratic form of government and they will need approval of their new mission.

This day in the Assembly Tamla started the session with the plan to go and explore the new Earth to find out what their former people of Millennia are in store for. Tamla was announced by the days Speaker and then she took the podium and said "thank you Mr. Speaker." After that she went on to say "fellow members I would like to have your attention please."

The shuffling around came to a halt as they all took their seats. Then after the house was quiet, she went on to say "thank you, as you know my daughter Brenda is leading the expedition to the new Earth, and earlier Commander Shasha and I were talking about how we would like to know how they are doing. So we meditated and came up with a plan to not only check up on them but to travel to the new Earth and find out what is in store for them there."

Taking a breath and a sip of the fine water provided from their equivalent of the Cascadian Mountains that are on Millennia. She went on and continued with this "I ask for your vote and approval of this plan."

Then the Speaker said "all in favor of the plan acknowledge with yea and all opposed with nay." The majority said yea but several said nay so the Speaker said "a sufficient number voting in the affirmative then the measure is passed."

The opposition spoke and said "we request a vote be tallied."

After the Speaker ordered a vote the plan was passed and Tamla was then free to seek council with the High Councilor Daanic of the Pleaides for the means of astral traveling there in a dream state. Nothing has changed they still must ask to either be visited by the High Council, or to travel there in their dreams.

Dinner was perfect as always, Shasha was so in her element in the kitchen. Now with life to continue on Millennia in the fourth dimension again she decided that now was the time to open up her own restaurant. No more cooking at home at least for five days a week and tonight was one of those days away from home.

Tamla showered in her office, changed her outfit, and then left work. Being as one of the people she rode the public transportation to Shasha's restaurant. Remembering how on Earth the politician's would ride around in limousines and right or wrong, they appeared to put themselves over the people. Shasha left the kitchen to join her for dinner. When Tamla arrived she was welcomed by her with a kiss on the check and then taken to their table. Shasha asked "how was your day?"

Now Shasha didn't have to attend the sessions in the Assembly unless needed and today her vote was by proxy. This freed her up to work at her own restaurant. Tamla responded to her and said "it was great, you voted for our plan to investigate the new Earth and to see how our people are doing. Well it passed by a large margin and we now need to talk with mom tonight about doing this."

"Okay, then let's enjoy dinner and talk about what we need to do tonight." She then poured some more white wine and continued with "do we need to ask the High Council for permission to astral travel on this?"

"I believe so, I'm positive she will grant us our wishes."

"Then why did we need to have the Assembly vote on it?"

"This is because we aren't going to do anything of this fashion without the approval of the Assembly."

"Right, I was just testing you." She said with a sheepish grin.

This evening they would ask together in meditation to speak with Daanic. During their sleep she visited them along with Jillela and a new friend named Ella. Ella was an alicorn and she seemed very familiar to both Tamla and Shasha. Jillela reached out for both of them and said "my two sweet granddaughters. Give this old dragon a hug."

A feeling of warmth from way back settled on Tamla, who said "oh grandma you always want hugs and we have them for you."

Shasha asked "are we going anywhere tonight?"

Daanic replied "no dear, this is just a pre visit; we are coming tomorrow after you wake up, so let's meet in my old gazebo. I'm starting to miss that old spot."

While looking at Ella this beautiful alicorn, Tamla said "mom, are you going to introduce us?"

"Sure, this is Ella she already knows who you are and soon you'll figure out who she is."

Shasha laughed and very quietly said to Ella "are you Coretta?"

Ella smiled and said "yes child I am."

They finished their dream and prepared for their visitors the next day. A dragon and an alicorn flew in with Daanic that day. They all had a wonderful visit in the gazebo. Daanic remembered her times there with Paul sipping wine and enjoying each other's company. Thinking of this she thought how strange it was that although it was a memory, she didn't feel any less happy today.

This visit was not only an excellent time to share with the people you love, but it was a very successful political meeting also. They all three agreed with Tamla and Shasha's plan, and looked forward to hearing back from them when they returned.

The night was very dark and there was a big storm on the way. Tamla was in bed before Shasha and eager to go on their journey. Shasha was brushing her teeth when this very large light erupted outside the window startled she said "what was that?"

Before Tamla could answer an incredibly loud sound of thunder cracked and Shasha screamed. Tamla laughed and said "my sweet angel that was lighting and the thunder."

"Thanks, I wish I could have prepared for that."

"True, but what matters is that we are ready for our journey tonight."

"Ready as I'll ever be. Turn off the light and let's go."

Don't you wish it was really that easy? Just decide you want to travel somewhere in your dreams and presto you're there! For them it is that easy, having mastered astral travel long ago. This is something to also be careful of because some people get so involved that they don't come back into their bodies again. Tonight we won't have that problem, these girls are masters!

"Hey, look there's the Milky Way galaxy, are we going to travel to the new Earth first?" Shasha was very excited to do this form of travel again.

"Yes we should gather all the information we can and then go back and observe our little girl Brenda."

"Okay, let's travel through the rings of Saturn. I've dreamed about that but never traveled there."

"Sure, let's go."

Flying in and out through their minds and sensing it all as if they were there physically. They both enjoyed doing this together and an experience like this with the person you love the most all these years is a very lovingly deep memory. Some time spent exploring Saturn and the other planets including the Sun was what they thought was an important part of their mission.

Tamla said "okay my little Dora the explorer let's head for Earth and check it out."

"If you insist, I guess I can pull myself away from this beautiful star."

Traveling to Earth they first stopped at the moon and noticed the base was still there on the dark side. Come to find out it was still manned and operational! Both performed a very gentle landing because they weren't sure who was still there. Then to their surprise they were both contacted telepathically by Amerorth.

"Hello you two and welcome to the moon of the new Earth."

Shasha said "I remember you, Papa Paul used to talk a lot about visiting you up here."

"Right you are he brought your dad up here too, many times. We boys had a great time studying and planning for the new technologies to come."

Tamla said "why didn't mom tell us you were here?"

"She didn't want to take away any surprises from you on this journey."

Both girls giggled like two teenagers and smiled at each other. It seemed that their learning would never end and that there will always be help where ever they travelled to.

"Okay Amerorth, do you want to tell us about the new Earth or should we find out for ourselves?"

Amerorth looked around and scratching his chin said "is that a rhetorical question?"

Shasha let out a loud laugh and said "ha, now that's funny. Tamla is full of those types of questions."

They bowed and said "good day sir" then flew down to visit the planet. As they were approaching the Earth to them it looked so alive and pristine. It didn't seem the same way as when they left. Swooping over the planet and taking notice of how the continents were formed, how it all looked very familiar. Shasha looked over at Tamla and said "now that we've flown around where do you want to stop?"

"How about we visit Alabama where we are from?"

"Let's go!"

Although the planet and time are real this is still all part of a dream. They can travel anywhere and anyway they want to. Then as they landed so to speak they looked around and didn't see any form of human life there. After searching the area for any trace of humans and finding none Tamla remembered a line from an old funny story that her dad told her when she was young, she said "let's blow this joint."

Full of wit and remembering the story Shasha replied "no girl, let's pass it on to the waitress."

"No I mean let's get out of here."

They both kissed and laughed at each other, moments like these really made their dreams feel real and in a special way they were.

So far, so good Tamla thought and she and Shasha agreed to travel the new Earth until they found some form of life. Flying over the Rockies and further west they spotted what looked like some type of settlement. Knowing that they were invisible they were able to fly down and see what the inhabitants were like.

As they grew nearer it became apparent that they were human. Now to find out if these humans were friendly was their next objective. First stop seemed to be some type of school. There the children were all dressed the same way and the teacher looked to be in the military. This was very disturbing to them both and they feared some type of a repressive civilization. Tamla was free to talk with Shasha since the people couldn't see or hear them. She said "this is very scary and we will need to gather more information."

"Yes it is and if this is a school then I'm concerned on what we will find next."

Discovering how and what the children were taught revealed that this new Earth was preparing for a war with the inhabitants south in Central America. The children were taught the basics, reading, writing and arithmetic. Then they were taught about building war machines, military tactics, and hatred of their so called enemy.

Moving on they entered into a type of market to buy goods. This place wasn't like the malls they remembered from their time on Earth. What they found seemed like what history recorded before of a war time economy. No items of pleasure, just clothes that were very plain, useful, and comfortable. Their foods were basic ones like bread, milk, and eggs.

Observing the people they all seemed to be very unsociable to one another. Men and women doing the shopping in fairly even numbers, so they thought that at least there seemed to be some equality. Even in this city of hate, sadness and unsocial behavior.

With a very heavy heart the girls left and regrouped into the streets and there looked around to see where they would go to next. Shasha grabbed Tamla's hand and said "dear this is a very depressing place, I don't know if my heart can go on from here."

"I know let's just stand for a few minutes and hold each other."

Waiting a few minutes and taking some deep breaths she then said "okay dear let's go to their political building and see what is going on."

Off they went not able to find this location by sight because their buildings didn't look like the ones from the former Earth. Travelling in and out of them they finally located the politicians. What they found were people arguing about the approaching war and there was certainly opposition to there being one. Shasha said "well at least it is some form of democracy and there are just as many women as men in their government."

"True and maybe that will help balance the hatred they seem to have for their fellow Earthlings."

As they were contemplating where to go to next, a voice came from above, and said "girls you need to leave and visit Brenda before you awake."

Recognizing who it was Tamla said "thanks mom, we are on our way."

Leaving the Earth with some knowledge of what their people will face was a little disturbing. Both talked about how they would talk with Brenda and inform her of what her people could encounter on Earth.

Approaching the moon they contacted Amerorth via telepathy and thanked him for all of his help. Shasha vowed that they would return soon and that they would let Paul and Cory know how things are on the moon base. That seemed to please him to no end for he missed his two friends.

Travelling at the speed of dreams can be however fast you imagine. Although they were in a hurry, both wanted to enjoy the beautiful universe that they swam in. Out of the Milky Way and searching for Brenda's ship, Shasha's heart was beating fast when she spotted it, and said "there, over there, the ship just went around that asteroid!"

Turning and moving faster Tamla smiled and said "yes dear let's get over there quickly."

As they arrived they entered into the ship and found the crew moving about doing their assignments. After some time of going through the ship, they finally made their way to the bridge, and there she was. Their little girl Brenda sitting in the Captain's seat where she belonged.

Talking to her First Mate James, Brenda said "how far are we from Earth?'

"According to our readings it seems that we have another five days of travel at our current speed Captain."

"Thank you Commander, take over the helm. I will be in the holodeck for some R & R."

Brenda left the bridge and her moms followed her to the holodeck. Both were excited after seeing how their daughter led her people. Although they were with her in the holodeck simulation, they noticed that they still could not communicate with her in this timeline. This really left them speechless in that they wanted to pass on the important information that they had learned.

Daanic watched as her girls struggled with not being able to warn Brenda and her people. Her heart was very heavy and she felt a sadness she hadn't experienced in a very long time. As she wept, a certain alicorn and dragon swooped in to comfort her. When her tears had come to an end she looked up to see them.

With her eyes red from tears, her mom changed from Jillela the dragon into Terames the elven human. This beautiful alicorn named Ella didn't change, she was just too beautiful, and the love she radiated was so powerful that no one else could enter into this area but them.

They both explained to her why this had to happen and she was briefed on how and what to say to Tamla and Shasha. Knowing that this was all part of the universal plan she did not argue, but felt how familiar it all was.

Shortly after mom changed back into a dragon, they both left and awoke. Daanic was now all alone and she wrote this song to later sing to her girls on Millennia.

Time Immemorial

Comprehend a pattern that stretches time and memory.
Not destroyed but exist through the fabrics of all sensory.
They are recorded in the records of all the great Masters.

A time in immemorial is out there for all who seek.
Listen to your Spirit, hear the call, you are not weak.

Many times a people have been given the keys of existence.
Learning in the cycle these Souls raise Love in persistence.
Struggles grow and the people will fall and be broken.

A time in immemorial is out there for all who seek.
Listen to your Spirit, hear the call, you are not weak.

A flower is cut after the petals have fallen, this is a plan.
Rebuild or regrow both are a process of plants and man.
Empires rise and fall to teach a lesson that is to be kept.

A time in immemorial is out there for all who seek.
Listen to your Spirit, hear the call, you are not weak.

Thus many tears are shed by the masters we know.
They are seeing this all play out in the one big show.
So being is our path that we are meant to follow.

A time in immemorial is out there for all who seek.
Listen to your Spirit, hear the call, you are not weak.

CHAPTER 6

Travelling through space at warp 8 they were anxious to arrive and land on Earth. After several months of space travel their memories of Tyreega, Hydrumn and Fyrooth were starting to fade. Unbeknown to them this is just how it's all supposed to be.

During the night the ships separated into seven fleets of several hundred each. This was something agreed upon in the charter from their home planets. This way each continent would be inhabited by them and the local resources would not be taxed too great.

We will follow Brenda's group for the foreseeable future. Her fleet will land in what is today the same area as Europe was on the previous Earth. They broke their fleet into three groups, one landing in the coastal region of Spain. The second landing in the area of Italy and the third which was Brenda's in the isles of the former United Kingdom.

The first thing to do now will be a reconnaissance of the area. Brenda gathered everyone together and said "my people as you are aware this is the planet Earth that we launched out from our homes to find. Now that we are here I ask of you to be patient and for us all to work together for the greater good. Our early days here will probably have many difficulties but when we work together we can achieve greatness. Now my first edict is to have a party of gratitude in one week."

Dozens of teams consisting of twelve members were sent out to gather all pertinent information. Some were gone more than a few days but thankfully all returned back safely and in time to attend the party. Reporting to the current government where Brenda gathered all the information she then disseminated it to each group to cultivate their plan for creating a new civilization. No human life was found in the area and the animals they could not communicate with them.

Brad was in charge of agriculture and he didn't even remember being a doctor before leaving on this journey. As far as he knew he was always a farmer. Receiving the information from Brenda he told her "we will create a co-operative of farmers that will produce the best fruits and vegetables while caring for this planet that is now our home."

Brenda acknowledged what he said by saying "I know you will Brad."

The information that they brought with them from their made up home was equivalent to the 21th century of Earth of its last cycle. For months they lived in the ships while they would slowly build their new settlements. The plan was for all to work, contribute and then share all of the bounty.

To make sure that the work was done properly the government assigned certain experts in their field to be in charge. The people worked hard and twice a month there was a community party for all to socialize and show their gratitude.

In their settlement the first one built was for the government. It was very large and was set up to do many things. Other than for government business it also processed and distributed food supplies. Shortly after this barns were built and some basic farm equipment was too. Schools and hospitals were built and then some commerce was started.

Not wanting to remember the warring planets they escaped from they decided the name of this settlement would be a new made up word. So the settlement was called Tarmish.

Today Brad wanted to show her the land he had picked to build their home and farm on. Brenda was always a country girl and now Brad was definitely a country boy. They didn't remember the home and farm they had before on Millennia but they both agreed that this is what they always wanted.

Getting a ride on the bus took a couple of days and even though she was their leader she refused to take any favors. He told her all about the land, water and the beautiful meadows that they would ride horses on once they located some. "Look, look this hill is where I want to build a power windmill generator and further down the river will be a little dam to generate energy too." Brad said.

"Oh Brad you sure are a fine example for our young people. You always think ahead and plan to be self-sufficient."

"I do, but I also want to share with as many of our people as I can."

They walked around looking at the areas where the different crops will be planted. Walking up the hill she could see how beautiful this land really was and later he showed her this area by a small creek where their house will be built. What a wonderful day to spend after all those months in space. She brought a picnic basket full of good food and they shared their bread with some squirrels they found.

They built a beautiful home, the community sprung up, and all went pretty well until one winter. The idea was that the whole community would all pitch it and work to put their goods in the storehouse for equal distribution. Now if you were a farmer or whatever trade you were, you were allowed to keep a little extra for yourself.

After several years this worked out pretty good it was not perfect but good. Over time the storehouse was less and less and some people didn't seem to work as hard because they would receive what they needed, no more or no less. Until this fateful winter, the rains that year were sparse, and the crops not so plentiful. Each of the last two years the storehouse had nothing left over from the last year and they would always count on the current year's harvest.

Neither Brenda nor Brad noticed what was going on until it was too late. The keeper of the storehouse told the governors that there was not enough food for the winter. They all made it through that winter but it was hard and many people were angry. Law enforcement was used to curtail some people that tried to break in to the storehouse and steal food. Brenda made sure that the food rationing applied to everyone. Even though she couldn't control the people, some had the good sense to always prepare for emergencies. Most of them were stars and helped the elderly and young children that needed nourishment the most.

During that winter not only was the food scarce but energy was in short supply because there were no oil or gas reserves. Even firewood piles were small and it was a cold winter. Brenda had everyone move into homes with many rooms and she closed down the smaller ones. This helped to preserve energy and keep everyone warm. This had a duel effect, it brought many people closer, but it did fuel hatred in others.

Brenda was so moved by this tragic time that seemed to bring out the best and worst in her people. She witnessed the hatred of them blaming others rightfully or wrongly, and to her it didn't matter which. What did most was that they as one people they were able to work it out, and become even stronger. The sad thing was that some people did separate and formed their own community. In her wisdom Brenda did not try and stop them however she did form a pact that they would protect each other and engage in fair trade.

Wanting to document her feelings she wrote her first song. Brenda did not know who her real grandmother was but she found this gift that came from her.

She reflected on the years or as they refer to them as seasons of the big red planet. In the writings that they brought, they were told that this planet only had one red planet that would warm them, and help their plants to grow. Where they were before these three planets each had as many as three moons and they were warmed by two smaller red planets.

All in all they were prepared for a lot of things on this new planet called Earth. But the one thing that wasn't included in the instructions was insurrection. It was bloody and it did cost many lives and even though Brenda, who tried to keep the peace, couldn't because of what had happened several years after they landed. Until some people seemed to change for the worse, and wanted to blame the government for any shortcomings there were.

After a few years of war Brenda was able to convince them that if they wanted to separate they could go in peace. This was their best option because they didn't want to live in the current society. Sad and heartbroken, all she could think about was this feeling of a place that she felt she lived in before, that was full of love for one another. Reading the songs of the laws and the Constitution from her home planet and not knowing that the writer was in fact her grandma. She grabbed her glass note pad and wrote this song.

Insurrections Lie

Work and toil are what we have to share if darkness rules
To never understand that we can share even as we get older
This light will shine and make itself known even to fools
By joining hand in hand and standing shoulder to shoulder

We are one and that one reigns in us all
Standing shoulder to shoulder
We are one and the one in us stands tall
Walking together, growing older

Turn away from loss and hate never to give in
Share with others and give what you have to find
Judgement of others only drags one down to sin
Rewards will come to fill your heart and mind

We are one and that one reigns in us all
Stand shoulder to shoulder
We are one and the one in us stands tall
Walking together, growing older

Running through your veins is a life waiting to reveal
Moving and flowing giving this body the energy to move

Breathe in deep then you know that all is not surreal
Learn living and loving as the dance for all to groove

We are one and that one reigns in us all
Stand shoulder to shoulder
We are one and the one in us stands tall
Walking together, growing older

Writing her first song was an experience she had never known before and this feeling will be one she will long for again and again. Now to get on with governing her people that she loved so much. Brad was her rock through these storms on Earth and she didn't know how she would have made it through without him so tonight she felt the need to let him know that.

"Brad, I'm home" she said after walking in but here was no answer and her heart was sad until she spotted him walking in through the back door. "Dear, I've been thinking about you all day at work."

He hadn't remembered her showing this kind of emotion before and he was puzzled by it and said "okay whoever you are what have you done with Brenda?"

She wanted to laugh but her heart was so happy that they made it through these rough times. She could only respond by saying "no it's just me, dear and I want you to know how much I appreciate you."

"Well you know I appreciate you even more."

Now she just sunk down in her chair and said "I know you do so much for me and all these years together I know it has helped make me who I am."

"Okay then, now let's go into the kitchen and clean this fresh produce I brought in from our personal garden."

Dinner was fresh, clean, green and very tasty tonight and they worked well together in the kitchen, cutting, cleaning, and searing some halibut that is in plenty supply. Their table looked like one that would grace a culinary magazine cover. Brad and Brenda didn't remember that they were both medical doctors in another life and that was just as well.

With the technology that they brought with them there was no need to reproduce on a large scale. With that said they did discuss having two children. Maybe it's not the natural way but with the advancements in science they could program the gender.

Brenda told Brad that their first baby will be whatever happens naturally. She didn't want their society to start choosing roles for the genders outside of what is natural.

Brad started to argue but instead said "but what if it's a girl, won't she follow you in politics?"

"Not necessarily because our children can do whatever they want to."

That put a smile on his face. Tonight after dinner, their discussion, and wine, they put in the order for their first baby.

These dangers were never something that could be prepared for like when this one hit the Separatists. Looking through the laws and Constitution this day the Assembly was rocked with the news. There was a massacre and it was the Separatists that were hit. Never wanting to have a military mindset, Brenda fought against building a large army. She remembered the desolation that their three planet's war had brought.

Sending a group out to investigate and gather much needed intelligence. This group was small and trained in the art of quiet and low visible movement. Waiting for the information the books were studied even harder and they found the agreement of how to handle hostile energies.

Reporting to the Assembly the team laid out all of their information gathered. First they were attacked by a technologically advanced people. The reasons for this attack weren't learned and that was something that needed to be determined. Second this attacking force came in quickly and seemed more interested in taking goods and killing anyone in the way. It was said that they didn't seem to go out of their way to kill, just only if you were in their way.

The first urgent order from the Assembly was to immediately send medicine, food, and a small force to help and protect them. Many were given first aide and if needed transported back to the hospital. This was all very hurtful knowing that these same people were involved in an insurrection where many were killed or injured. Now they are attacked by an unknown force and after seeing some of the children dead or injured, Brenda pledged to never settle their differences with force again.

Months went by and still no word of the attackers yet. A new industry sprang up to build military vehicles and armaments in Tarmish. Knowing how dangerous this could be the Assembly still voted to do it, and to build up their military. With some careful planning and debating there were safeguards added to protect from turning into a war economy.

Flying machines were designed and built then sent out to search the planet for these warring people. To not be seen these inhabitants were located using heat sensors from far up in the air. The machines would then land, the teams will assemble, trek across the countryside to locate the attackers, and to perform a well needed reconnaissance. After this information was gathered they were to do a 180 degree turn and be picked up halfway on their previous route. All the teams made it back except for one that was captured and couldn't be rescued at this time. After the extraction of the other teams, loads of rockets, and small arms fire filled the skies. No planes were shot down but some did sustain a lot of damage. These attackers were just what they were and that was attackers!

Welcoming their people home Brenda and the military intelligence committee were anxious to find out what was learned. Also they were very concerned about the team that was captured. By accessing all the information it will help them materialize two plans. One plan will be to recuse the team and the other is to arrange some type of meeting with the attacker's leaders if possible.

A private meeting to come up with the two plans was in session. This meeting involved all of her advisors and the representatives from each of the townships. Here they used the old knowledge of getting the brains in one room and combine their energy to perform magic.

Talking with her top advisor and his name is Herthro she asked him "do you believe we can break into their town and free our people or should we send them a message to meet and negotiate?"

"I think the wise thing to do would be to negotiate and try to establish some form of mutual peace."

The group all weighed in, some agreed to negotiate and others added that by building their military it would help reinforce their power to defend themselves. On and on they went back and forth proposing this and arguing about that. All the while she was being watched by her moms and grandma's from an unknown dimension.

Daanic looked at her friend Jenny and said "our granddaughter is a very wise leader. I remember when my mom said that she will be greater than us all one day."

"I couldn't agree more, she seemed to just be a natural born leader. Have you heard the first song she wrote? I thought it was very good."

Tamla and Shasha stood there focused on Brenda like a laser beam. Both smiling and holding each other's hand. Daanic was told telepathically that Brenda will be visited by a dragon named Jillela and later an alicorn named Ella both in her dreams.

Turning from Brenda Daanic asked the girls "how are things on Millennia?"

Shasha said "we are fine, it's different with Brenda and all the others gone."

Tamla thought on it and said "yes and we are making large strides with learning about all the other inhabitants now that they are represented in the Assembly."

Jenny gave them both a hug and said "you two are always in my heart."

Daanic not wanting to be left out moved in and got her hugs too from all three ladies. She then said "let's blow this joint."

Jenny laughed and said "why do you always temp the girls with those catchy lines?"

"I'm just trying to keep them on their toes."

CHAPTER 7

Even though their life on Earth has been rewarding and very difficult, one of the things the people from Tyreega, Hydrumn and Fyrooth insisted on was to assimilate all people into one. This they knew was the only way they would survive in their new home environment.

As Daanic and the girls finished checking up on Brenda they felt the need to visit the other settlements around the Earth. Asia would be the next stop, and aside from the extreme cold weather, the settlement there was doing well. They had established a very useful fishing industry and stored plenty of vegetables for the winter months. Something else they did was to create a rather large dome to grow plants during the cold months. Seeing this, Jenny's words described it as "quite impressive."

Off they went to Australia to see how the people were doing down under. Their ships landed on the western side of the continent and had to deal with the harsh summer weather. Building ships quickly became their industry along with fishing. They did find some local people and were able to make friends. These people weren't concerned about material things, so therefore they were generally very peaceful.

Tamla said "so far so good except for Brenda's people's trouble with the attackers, the rest seem to be doing quite well."

"I couldn't agree more my dear, and I do hope that Brenda can work with those people." Shasha said while looking out at the ocean.

"Well let's go and find out what's happening in Africa." Daanic whispered to Jenny.

Here their ships landed in the jungle and although there were plenty of fruits and vegetables, there were some animals that were very dangerous. Each group was equipped with volumes of information to learn from. Then once they determined the location of where they were it sure came in handy. Here the temperatures were mostly warm and for their own protection they built the settlement on a mountain range surrounded by water.

South America was by far the most established and they landed in the area of Machu Picchu. This was very interesting that where they landed was a previous ancient site, but there were no people in the area. Here there was some very positive energy that encouraged them to build some fantastic things.

Last but certainly not least was North America and what they found there was very disturbing. Arriving at the landing site they only found the ships and while searching and searching for the people all that they found was many burnt ships and dead bodies everywhere. As they entered the ships they noticed that anything of value was taken. Crying and bemoaning the fact that they couldn't warn them Tamla and Shasha were sad and angry.

Shasha said "why in the name of all that's right and just could we not warn our people of these war mongers?" Stomping in her dream state she looked at Daanic very puzzled and asked her "why, why, why can you tell me?" Daanic walked up to give her a hug and she pushed her away and said "what the hell is happening are they going back in time to a hostile Earth?"

Daanic said "dear I am hurting just like the rest and I don't know all of the reasons except that the Earth is in another cycle and Brenda's generation is starting this one."

Tamla took her by the hand and with tears streaming down her face she buried her head into Shasha's breast.

After gathering their composure and then trying to imagine the best it was time to go find them. Tamla and Shasha knew just where to go because they were there before. Seeing the cities from afar Daanic prepared her heart for the worst.

Jenny not remembering that this was a dream whispered "we need to go in there quietly and find out what has happened to our people."

The girls laughed and Daanic put her arm around her best friend and said "my dear we are ghosts to them, they can't see or hear us."

"Oops you are right, what was I thinking?"

Flying into the city, and in and out of the buildings, they were noticing how unhappy these people were. Jenny was especially disturbed when she noticed how the people went even further backwards over human rights. They watched as the children were taught in school how they should live in negative ways.

This society was now very patriarchal in that men held all the military, political and clerical positions. Not to mention men owned and ran all the businesses and the women couldn't even vote anymore. Women had three choices, homemaker, nurse or teacher. Tamla said "we need to do something about these men it's appalling what they are doing."

Jenny then asked Daanic "what can we do about them, Your Grace?"

Daanic was taken back because outside of the Council Jenny never addressed her in this way. So with a very small encouraging smile she said "I'm not sure but you can bet we will ask Jillela and Ella as soon as possible."

Knowing that there was nothing to do here it was decided to leave and astral travel back to the Pleiades and Millennia.

Wanting to make peace in the worst way possible Brenda knew this was going to be tricky. After reading the laws on how to deal with these hostile forces, she sat down by the lake and formulated a plan to make peace with the enemy. She didn't like using the word enemy but for now they certainly were just that for attacking her people outside the settlement, and then capturing one of her reconnaissance teams. With that said she knew this was an act of war.

Pulling up the map of the information gathered from the recon on her glass pad, she thought first there will need to be a diversion, and then a mission to rescue the captured team. Now what will they do for a diversion? That she didn't know yet, but tomorrow she will request some ideas from the Assembly.

During this diversion the rescue team will be stationed a couple of clicks (a click is a kilometer) outside the city walls near one of the rivers leading in. A night with no moon will be needed to help them stay unseen. The day before another recon will need to be done to ascertain what means they will use to enter the city. If there are no mines or obstacles in the river then an underwater entry will work the best.

Taking a sip of tea and some deep breathing in a lotus position, there she decided to meditate for a while. Clearing her mind and releasing any stress from this situation. After several minutes her lungs felt energized, she opened her eyes, and started back working on the plan.

Although she doesn't remember her great grandpa Connor talking about the war in the Pacific, and how he was a paratrooper there would have given her this idea. Maybe it was in her subconscious mind all along. One of the diversions will be a large scale military airborne force on the other side of town, several clicks away at least. They will draw away the enemy's major military force and then leave the city less guarded.

Once inside her people will need to find out where the team is being held. This could take some time and a full scale plan of deception will need to be made. Probably something in the way of the team blending in with the locals and this will need to be done while they search the town. To keep the enemy out of the city their airborne unit will perform maneuvers drawing them further and further away.

Compiling all of this information she realized that there was much more needed to be done. Like an exit plan for the airborne unit and the rescue team with their people now in safely. It was getting late and her eyes were not staying open, so leaving the solitude of the lake, she returned home to Brad, and a restful night's sleep.

Waiting for her to return Brad knew that she had a heavy burden on her heart. Even though he wanted to help her, he had learned that she would always find her inner strength by being alone and in meditation. Having brewed some chamomile tea for her to sip on and relax before bed was just what she needed. Not to mention the neck and back message he would give her. Kissing his hands she said "Brad you are so good to me."

"My darling you have a lot to deal with and we all need to do our part and support each other."

"Thanks this tea and message are just what I need."

Waking up the next morning Brenda felt like she traveled somewhere in her sleep but wasn't sure where. With no experience in lucid dreaming she made a note to investigate this. Rolling over to say good morning to Brad and noticing that he wasn't there. She then said "well I guess he wakes up with MR rooster."

Moving downstairs and smelling the fresh black tea she just took in a whiff. Brad heard her walking down the stairs and he left the kitchen to meet her by the door way. There he said "good morning sunshine."

"What smells so good besides the tea?"

"Well I made a fruit plate and some fresh rice cereal with nuts."

She smiled at him and poured the tea while he prepared the plates. Walking outside to make good use of the morning sun they felt fresh and very thankful today. After some tea and fruit their conversation began. She showed him what she had come up with regarding the plan so far. He gave her some ideas on how to achieve the exit plan and after writing them down she added a few of her own. A few passionate kisses and they were off to do their work of the day, she to the Assembly and he to the farm.

Looking over and over what she had compiled so far the group worked and worked to mold it into a comprehensive plan.

Stopping for some group meditation that they really needed, which now took them into their lunch break. Returning from lunch Brenda announced that she felt that she could put this together in private.

Alone in her office and feeling a sense of being communicated with by her elders but not sure who they were. Breathing in deep and closing her eyes she leaned her head back and said "whoever you are I can feel your presence and I love you very much." Waking up she then picked up her tablet to write this.

Friends and Foes

In this world full of fear and lust
We come to be hopeful of that day
Our Spirits are eternal and are just
A day that we will all come to say

This day we are attacked by a foe
Things that were ours they took
A people that we didn't even know
By night they killed and forsook

Peace is what we teach
Love is who we are
Never turn to hate
A people near or far

Plans to free our loved ones
Seeing our foe has them in chains
To travel where the river runs
Paratroopers descending like rain

Searching in the city all about
Their army now away from town
They are north of town so we get out
The rest of the plan to go down

Peace is what we teach
Love is who we are
Never turn to hate
A people near or far

North we will move them far away
Their troops leave the city alone
Free to rescue our people today
On our trucks we headed home

Peace is what we teach
Love is who we are
Never turn to hate
A people near or far

The mission was a success with only a couple of glitches. There was some mortar fire from the enemy on the airborne unit and it was detected early. The mortar rounds where shot out of the sky or the troops just moved out of their range. The rescue team made it in with no problems and blended in with the locals. Not sure if it was a matriarchal society or not, but they made sure that the team was made up of women, and young men who were too young for the army. Brenda wrote a letter to their leader requesting a meeting to negotiate a peaceful settlement to these hostilities.

Just like in the laws from their planets (Millennia) she followed them. One part of the plan was to "plant a seed, that one day it will grow." Not only did she write a very cordial letter but she also offered some gifts in a package and now to see if the seeds will grow into a big peaceful tree.

CHAPTER 8

Daanic was back at the High Council and she had many questions for her mom. Controlling her anger from what was happening on Earth she calmly asked instead of insisting on some answers. She made her request known and when Ringo returned with the answer she was pleased. Both Ella and Jillela were busy and understood that Daanic was upset so they cut short what they were doing and arrived at the High Council the next day.

"Well hello my daughter, how are you doing?"

Daanic smiled at her mom who is now a beautiful dragon and said "I love you mom even now that you are a dragon I still want a hug."

Ella the alicorn was nearby and watched them exchange their pleasantries. The High Council was not in session so the chamber belonged to them. Having the chamber all to their selves was good because Ella and Jillela brought with them a strange looking stone. At least that's what Daanic thought this strange smooth oval shaped blueish green orb was. Reaching for it her mom said "don't touch it because it's obtaining the memories we programmed for it to use."

"What is it?"

Ella said "it's a device that will help us answer your questions, we hope."

The lights dimmed and the orb began to heat up and turn red then purple. A hum started to emanate and the sound became higher and higher until it reached a very high level then it just stopped. When the sound ended and the orb was a bluish green colour again, seconds later it changed to pure white, and then some white circles projected up in a vertical direction. They grew larger as they went up, until they ended and just fell down like a dove descending to the earth.

First a very large 3 dimensional Earth appeared above it. It was simply beautiful and Daanic was mesmerized by it. Then it showed an area of the planet that Brenda was on. Moving in closer she could see the people and what was happening. Her granddaughter was so happy she had three children from age four to seven. Watching her she could see that everything will work out and there was so much more to watch.

The picture moved out and went to a few areas of the world. One of them was in the continent of Africa and there was a war. Even though she made peace with the people that attacked them, Brenda sent an airborne unit to help hold a strategic point in this war. This airborne unit was also there to help the army negotiate with the enemy.

Daanic looked at them both and said "it looks like the way Earth was when I was there."

Ella spoke directly to her and said "my dear granddaughter don't you understand this?'

"No I don't think I do understand can you elaborate on it for me?"

"This is an ongoing process of ascension of the Spirit. Brenda proved herself on Earth in her last life and she then transcended to Millennia to perfect her Light energy some more. During that time she also made a change in her profession from a doctor to a politician. Now both have their redeeming qualities and she needed to become a politician to then be the leader she now is."

"So she is a Wayshower like I was on Earth?"

Jillela felt it was time for her to take over. She said "Not exactly". There was a pause because even though she took over the conversation from Ella she wasn't sure how to say the next words.

Daanic said "mom were you going to say something else?"

Knowing that the next phase of information shouldn't be given to Daanic yet Ella said "that's all we can say about that right now."

"Okay then can you tell me how we can help Brenda and her people?"

Ella looked over at Jillela and gave her a nod of approval.

Jillela then said "Brenda will need to ask the Father of Spirits (which is pure and undefiled Love) for assistance. Then Tamla and Shasha will visit her in a dream."

Pondering and trying to analyze what she said Daanic knew that to reach Tamla and Shasha fully in understanding that a song was needed. Goodbyes, hugs and kisses were given and the dragon and alicorn flew off back to their work in the universe. Not wanting this moment to slip away Daanic wrote this on her energy pad aka ePad.

Knowledge of Love

Wander through the universe to know
Find love and hate in all that is around
Look up, look down, look everywhere!
Need, want, see this energy it will grow

Let the power of Love reveal
Knowledge that Love is real!
Sharing, caring and believing

Energy of hate becomes too great
Remove from the waters this fear
Reject judgement and all for gain
Unburdened and free to meditate

Let the power of Love reveal
Knowledge that Love is real!
Sharing, caring and believing

Your voice is heard so don't fight
Deep into your soul you'll find
Your Spirit wants to return
To the universe of Love and Light

Let the power of Love reveal
Knowledge that Love is real!
Sharing, caring and believing
This Love we now will seal

Hoping that this song will help them understand, maybe when Brenda calls the girls will sing it to her. All Daanic could do now was wait for them to contact her again because this connection only goes one way and they must do just that for her to visit them.

They didn't forget about Daanic and Brenda but things were busy on Millennia and there were lots of things to attend to. Living in an almost perfect world will tend to confuse some lines of business and pleasure. Tamla was very alert to how times on the previous Earth would go through boom and bust periods. Knowing this the laws that were written mostly by her mother should help them prevent just that.

Enjoying their life together but aware of the troubles Brenda was going through made for some complications. The inhabitants on Millennia are now looking to build an economy and some wanted to pattern it as a *laissez-faire* one and others more of a government run economy. Following the great Margo's (Daanic) laws Tamla convinced both sides to cooperate.

Tonight they were talking after dinner about their daughter and how they could help her. Sadly sipping on some of the fine wine her daddy Paul put together thinking about Brenda's troubles. Tamla said "when we were with our moms they told us that they would find out how we could help Brenda. I just wonder when they will let us know how?"

"Dear don't we have to ask to visit them in our dreams or to have them come here?"

"Yes we do and tonight in our dreams let's do just that."

With her heart filled with hope, Shasha smiled and said "I am so confident that before we wake up we will have our answer."

Sure enough in their dreams they travelled to the High Council and were greeted officially by the High Councilor herself.

Ell and Jillela were there in their official capacity as Ambrosia and Terames, both in their full gowns.

"Wow this is great to see you both dressed in your High Councilor gowns" Shasha said to Ambrosia and Terames.

"Yes, and it's good to be Ambrosia once again."

Daanic was listening and watching as her girls were excited to see them again. She waited for a few more minutes and said "okay let's get to the answering of your question."

"So mom, are you going to tell us how to help Brenda?"

"Yes, first I will sing you a song and then answer any questions after that."

Listening to her sing the song she wrote, with some of the most heavenly music and sound. They were mesmerized by it all and then the questions began to flow. Daanic then sat down and said "yes Shasha what is your question?"

"This song is very nice and I loved it. So, my question is this; is it written for us or Brenda? It sounds like it is for her so how does she hear it? I mean…"

Tamla broke in and said "right, I love the message but it doesn't seem to help us?"

"Okay so it doesn't really give you any instructions on how to help her. What it does is to confirm how the universe works."

Shasha then looked over at Ambrosia and Terames and said "what do you two have to say about this?"

Daanic quickly thought of a way to cut off this type of questioning. So she answered her by saying "my dear Terames and Ambrosia are the ones that I went to for this answer. So I am telling you what they had to say about this."

Tamla just chuckled and said "chain of command, we must remember that we all play our part in it. We are sorry to seem unappreciative but we are concerned for our baby girl."

Terames said "that's okay we more than understand and know this that she and her people will be fine in the end. Remember we always are taken care of and these times of trouble are meant to help us in our ascension."

Daanic then smiled and said "thank you, Your Grace, you are so kind and we love you both very much..."

Shasha spoke with tears and said "yes, and I am so sorry to question your feelings. You all have been such an inspiration to me and Tamla."

Before Tamla could speak Daanic raised her hand for her to be quiet so she could say "Brenda will contact you both and when she does you will get your chance to help her."

The meeting was concluded then the girls left by waking up in the morning. Ambrosia and Terames both gave Daanic the rest of the plan, showing her more info from the orb, and then answering her questions.

Not being quite satisfied with the answers Tamla said to Shasha while still in bed. "I don't have the energy to go on today knowing that we can't help Brenda until she seeks us first."

Always the one to help her friend, partner, and Councilor, Shasha then said "you will get up and we will face the day together. We must be strong and we must help the people here while waiting for our daughter to contact us."

Leaning over to kiss her Tamla said "you are my rock of Gibraltar."

And that's the way it was for now. They would just have to be patient and continue on with their lives on Millennia.

With the team rescued from their enemy Brenda waited to hear from their leader. It wasn't long, that three days later an envoy approached their settlement under a type of peace symbol. At least that's how they perceived it to be and so they met with them outside the protection area. Introductions were made and then their leader gave Brenda's top aide a tablet with a message to give her.

This visiting group turned and headed back home while Brenda's people went back to their settlement. Heading straight for the door of the Assembly, Herthro couldn't get the information to Brenda fast enough.

He approached her short of breath and said "Your Grace this hasn't been looked at by anyone yet so I felt it was important that you see it firsthand."

"Thank you Herthro, now you and I will see it together."

The message was from the Great General Barborda who seemed more than full of himself. After reading the introduction of how great he was they got to his message and in it he said that he wasn't at all impressed with their rescue attempt. Even though it was successful to them he believed that they wouldn't be able to pull that off a second time. Trying to be serious they both couldn't help but laugh especially when he asked who their real leader was. He went on to ramble about how a woman couldn't possibly be able to lead their people.

Brenda put down her copy and said "whew what a lot of hot air. How do you think we should handle this?"

"Well that is a good question and my first thought was this; I think we need to prepare for war. At the least we need to prepare to defend ourselves."

"Okay my friend then let's brainstorm and come up with some ideas."

"Your Grace let us meditate first because I feel so much negative energy after reading his remarks."

"Another good idea, I see why I keep you around." Then she winked.

For the next 18 minutes they did just that and in her chamber, there was a place for them to relax. The lights were dim and with some mantra music and incense burning the time was well spent.

Brenda awoke and said "I have an idea to deal with our narcissist ruler and that is we will prepare for war and at the same time we will secretly send his people gifts."

"How will we know what type of gifts to send?"

"We will send some teams in to find out what they need."

"Your Grace, do you mean to observe from a distance?"

"Not really, I think we should have some of our people sneak in under cover just like before."

"Okay but, that could be risky and might get them captured."

"Herthro it's just an idea."

He laughed and said "you're right, I'm sure we will come up with a plan that will limit those risks."

Some time went by and they were very successful in gathering this information. Brenda and her people sent in a lot of supplies to help the less fortunate of the enemy's people. They were very careful not to seem too knowledgeable of their needs.

Over the next few years there was peace between them and their neighbors. The people that left the settlement before started to return little by little and the hard feelings were almost completely gone. So Brenda felt good enough about this to write another song.

Good Neighbors

Being the only ones can be a true blessing

Discovery is just around the bend of time
Another people you find without guessing
Push the limits of love and then you shine

Love thy neighbor is the Master's call
Treat them as you would yourself
Loving and caring you then stand tall

Planting seeds of Love in many a row
Giving good food and watering them
Allowing Love plenty of time to grow
The root of kindness will sprout in

Love thy neighbor is the Master's call
Treat them as you would yourself
Loving and caring you then stand tall

Prepare to be rejected many times over
Suffer arrows of fear and misunderstanding
Then their heart melts and becomes sober
To love is always the seeds of our planning

Love thy neighbor is the Master's call
Treat them as you would yourself
Loving and caring you then stand tall

Herthro liked this song very much and this inspired him to write this letter to her.

"*To my esteemed High Councilor Brenda,*

This letter is written just for you. I know that I do not always tell you my feelings for you as my friend and as my leader on a day to day basis. The feelings that I do share are not great enough or expressed enough to capture the magnitude of your worth to me and to our people.

When you guided us on our old home planets to come up with the plan for leaving before the elders destroyed them. You then helped direct us in building the ships and communicating with the people from the two other planets. How you managed to get us all talking and working towards a common goal is still a feat that can't be explained and that just scratches the surface of what you have done.

Our travels in space weren't easy either, there you kept us sane. When many people started to get a "cabin fever" you then brought all the leaders together and implemented games for us to play to "take our minds off being "cooped up". Knowing that we would separate into seven groups and land on this new planet called Earth. That's where you let us know that the future is all in front of us and that we are equipped with the tools and knowledge we need.

Sure this letter is getting long and if you were to write it, it would then be a song. I added that to make you smile because I want you to know how much you've meant to me all these many years. So now back to the letter of your story.

Landing on Earth was certainly stimulating and more than just exciting. Our ships landed in an area close to a rocky coast where the climate is mild and a little cool at times. After landing you immediately sent out our teams to do a reconnaissance of the area. When they returned you put together a plan of how we would create a settlement as a co-op to work and share with all. Not knowing how long this would last this system of collaboration slowly turned on us and we were faced with a hardship.

Not to be discouraged you arranged for us to share all that we had with each other to make it through the winter. Although some rejected most or all of this and began to cause an insurrection you did not meet them with the same negative energy. Instead you attempted to talk with them and try to work this out diplomatically.

After many injuries from their eagerness to try and conquer the government you rallied our forces enough to push them out. There we began to negotiate with them and made an agreement to be allies and trade with one another. That's when you made your appeal to the Assembly of the justness and future of keeping them as part of our community and on the Assembly.

When our separatists were attacked by a hostile force you immediately went to help them. Food and supplies flowed into their settlement and the badly injured were brought back to our hospitals. After that time our two peoples became one again. Because of this attack you asked the Assembly to send a couple of teams out to find these hostile people. This was done to gather information so we can then assess the danger we might be in.

When one of our teams was captured you then put together a rescue plan that you shared with the Assembly. With only some minor changes the plan was carried out and the team rescued. Also in this plan you had left a "gift basket with a message to their leader." After only a few days you received a response from him and even though it wasn't friendly at all you still saw the benefit in working towards making peace with them.

Now today we are working towards a peace treaty with these hostile people and after years of sneaking in supplies and knowledge to their people we believe they are ready to change their government. I close with this one last breath of my Spirit to give to you. I will follow you wherever you choose to lead me my Sovereign Queen.

Your friend and follower forever,
Herthro

CHAPTER 9

Years go by and Tarmish has grown into a very progressive city. Energy is free, food is plenty and organically grown. Employment is full where people do the type of work they enjoy. The monetary system is sound and it provides a means of currency for trade. Over the decades of life there have been several skirmishes with the enemy of Sorentito.

Trying to balance a collaborative economy with a military one to defend against the Sorentitians hasn't always been easy. She did her best to hold it together but in her awareness she could see that it was slipping away. Brad and Brenda did have children, a boy, and a girl. Both are now adults and their daughter is a doctor of medicine, while their son chose to be an engineer building aircraft.

Tarmish has been in touch with the other five settlements of their people. Learning that one of the seven was captured and their ship destroyed a very long time ago. The people of Sorentito have also been in contact with the other peoples of Earth that were here before Brenda's people arrived. They have been working on a plan of attacking their so called "invaders" and conquering them.

Information has been gathered for many years about this by her people called *Tres Vagans* which loosely means three planets. A meeting has now been called for the six settlement nations around the world to address the future of an impending war. Since Brenda has been the leader of the Tres Vagan people from day one, even long before they left their planets to come to Earth, it was she that arranged the time and the place. Doing a study from years of data collected it was decided that the nation in South America would be the location. It was far away from any possible enemy and the high altitude made for a good strategic defensible location.

Communications were clandestine and also jammed from being intercepted during the last decade. Each nation flew in the cover of night and all planes had stealth technology. The nations did not bring their top leaders, but brought the number two in command, to avoid something happening to their leaders. Each one was required to bring an elite military group the size of a battalion, and this gave them a force the size of a fully complete brigade.

Machu Picchu is a beautiful place to be and the second in command felt very privileged to be there. Herthro was in charge as the acting High Councilor and he had his orders from Brenda. All the leaders were settled in and the military had posted their perimeter of protection. So Herthro said "fellow Tres Vagans I welcome you to this meeting. Let us first watch this information that our High Councilor put together."

The room went dark and the orb in the middle of the floor came alive then a light beamed out vertically. When the light particles fell they then became a three dimensional image complete with sound, motion, and vibrations. In the movie they were shown the plans that Brenda had put together. First it started with a specific area of the world that was Europe. Brenda did an assessment and determined that the forces in that nation and the terrain were more suited to accommodate a large battle.

In the movie, the leaders were shown how each nation will leave behind a force, that's capable enough to hold off an attacking one, until reinforcements can arrive. The other nations will then send the bulk of the military to Tarmish for training and equipment. Once there they are to be shown how each of the nation's military will be separated into units. Some of these units are to be specialized, while the other ones will be conventional forces. As time went on in the movie they would see how the Tres Vagan military would merge and become a formidable force.

Once this was established and all that watched did seem to like and understand what had just happened. Some would say to each other how it reminded them of a time before when they left their homes to travel to Earth. Developing these forces will take some time and the location they picked is very large. There was a naval force with aircraft carriers and submarines. The idea was to not fight sea battles and if attacked the planes and submarines would defend the carriers.

Taking it all in they could envision a large scale war and Brenda was more than aware of the enemy's plans. They were building a very large force of tanks, planes, and ships mostly based on the eastern coast of North America. Brenda was concerned with an attack into South America but after noticing the size and travel capacities of their ships, she was certain that they were planning to launch out, and attack another continent.

On the safe side there will be many Engineers stationed in the southern Central American and northern South American regions. Once there they will build multiple obstacles and have many bridges primed with explosives in preparation of an invasion. The leaders were very impressed with this type of planning as to address many contingencies. "Wow" one said when they saw and heard the explosion it was amazing! All you could hear said was "what was that, what was that." Before they could ask again several planes swooped in and roared right over them. It felt that real and looking through the smoke they noticed the bridge was gone!"

Right in the command center they were in this movie and Brenda was watching as the commanders would give updates on the progress of the air strikes. A very large world map was illuminated in this command center and constantly updated. They could see forces moving around mostly in the eastern part of Europe. The colours were blue for them and red for the enemy. The ground war seemed to be mostly slow but the airstrikes from bases and carriers were constantly moving. To watch an anticipated war right in front of your eyes is quite remarkable.

As the battle lines would move the forces of Tres Vagans would avoid contact at all costs. The goal was not to lose many people in an attempt to just conquer land. Being a peaceful people the Tres Vagans practiced good vibrations and took time to meditate on what to do next. That is until enemy tanks were moving towards Tarmish! They were so quiet waiting, watching and gasping at the thought of their city falling. Resistance that was given was that their forces would strike and then retreat over and over again. None of this made sense, where was the air support and why did they not do everything to defend their city?

The movie stopped and the lights slowly came on. The leaders of the nations all stood and looked at one another. Some were heard to say "does this mean we will be defeated?" Others said "this is very disturbing and it seems our forces are letting them take the city." Herthro sat and watched all the while knowing the plan. He didn't laugh or smile because their reactions will be analyzed later. Once everyone sat back down and were quiet he stood and said "leaders these events are very disturbing so let me suggest some meditation time.

"Whew that was needed they were so swimming in negativity." Herthro said to himself while watching and waiting for someone in the group of five to try and redirect this energy but it didn't happen. Now he was ready to show them the rest of movie. Then the orb turned back on and the lights in the room went dark as the vertical light emanated up and slowly fell down. As the movie began it picked right up where the city was being sieged. There was a battle and the enemy just kept advancing forward with still no air support from Tres Vagans.

Conversations went on and on seemingly waiting for their city to fall, however it never seemed to happen soon enough, although they all were more than aware that it would. Questions came to Herthro from all directions and now they were more intelligent. Like "are we not giving air support because we want the city to fall?" Herthro didn't answer except to nod in their direction approvingly.

What they didn't know was that Herthro was in control of when the city would fall. He waited for their questions and statements to turn more in the direction of what was going to happen. Each time someone would say "this is a trap!" or "we are luring them in aren't we?" He would see these changes in the movie happen per their words until finally he stopped the movie. Then he stood up and they were confused. You could hear then say "what is going on? Did we piss him off?" Herthro was laughing so loud that they all sat down and became very quiet because they thought he was so mad.

He then looked around and smiled and said "I'm not pissed off or angry or mad. If fact I'm very pleased with the conclusions you have all come to." Stunned they were, very happy the energy in the room was something that Brenda told Herthro to try and bring out.

Someone said "can we see what happens?"

Herthro said to him "that all depends on this room."

Another leader asked "what do you mean?"

"It depends on your collective thought energies."

Then throughout the room you could hear "ah now I see" and then it was quiet. The movie started and the city fell and what they saw was just what they imagined. There were no people in the city just machines firing weapons by remote control. As the enemy tanks rolled in, in triumph, the soldiers marched in, and they moved the ruble in order to formed into their positions. Their commander flew in on a very elaborate aircraft one that could land and lift vertically. He stepped out and his uniform was full of medals that made Napoleon look like a private.

Winds blew into the city and they were very cold, very cold indeed and these conquerors looked puzzled because after being there they noticed there were NO PEOPLE! The whole room laughed because they knew that they were controlling the whole situation and it felt so good to do this. One of the leaders was so excited that she stood up during the movie and said "we can decide the fate of the world!"

The meeting was concluded, so later we shall see how well they did with this new found power of conscious thought. Nothing is perfect but what the leaders learned did help them with the up and coming war. What was very instrumental was their ability to sway the outcome of many battles. This didn't cause them to win the war but after a few years there was a truce signed. Thankfully the enemy grew tired of not winning many battles and could see that if they continued they would probably loose.

Lines were drawn and even though the enemy signed a truce they didn't want any part of trade or relations with the Tres Vagan people. The six nations held their current settlement areas and the city of Tarmish was now safe from any danger of an attack. The one aspect of defense that Brenda did was to combine the police and military as one agency. This saved money and allowed them to rotate the units around and become more known by the people. It also was a way to give them a break from the domestic problems of the day.

War is never something you want to deal with and the Tres Vagans did just what they needed to end it. Life will continue for Brad and Brenda who are ready to enjoy their family now that they are grandparents. It's time to let this planet enjoy her children that came from afar now that peace is in the air and it is beautiful.

Generations have come and gone where many things on Earth have transpired. There are now cities and nations that are populated by hundreds of millions of people. There are also the other people that were there before. The average life span is around seven hundred years for the Tres Vagan people. Early on the settlements were small and able to use renewable energy from around them like solar, wind, and power plus now they have engineered other natural sources.

As the cities grew and the two peoples had disputes over territory there were some little wars. None of these wars lasted more than a few years and were kept to a local area, they never went worldwide. In this pattern of a war every so often it made the people aware of how needless war was.

With the Tres Vagan people being as peaceful as they could be and having volumes of information on many subjects. They had an advantage over the other peoples on Earth in that they these people did not possess the knowledge of the universe. Therefore in the span of a few hundred years the Sorentito people did not learn from them and because they rejected their attempts to unite.

During harsh winters and even large scale droughts the Tres Vagans would send the leaders wheat with other foods to help the people of Sorentito. These leaders would take care of themselves first and then the people and they would not let them know where it came from. As time went on the Sorentito's became less and less prosperous their leaders did not know what to do and they didn't want to ask the Vagans for any help.

A war economy was what they built and King Barborda would tell them how the Vagans are just waiting to attack. He would have the children learn lies about how awful these people are and that they must learn how to defend themselves. The people would continue to work for the government and all communications were restricted to only what the king would approve. This made for generations of people stuck in a type of darkness that they could not find the light.

Attempting to conquer some of the *Tres Vagan* cities and constantly being repelled. The king could see that his people were getting angry because of a lack of food and the supplies were not keeping up with the demand. Their way of farming for the government and lack of knowledge on the proper ways of managing the land took a mighty toil.

Having a large cache of war machines and soldiers at his disposal king Barborda started to blame his allies and then attacked some of them. The battles were very costly and brutal and the king's forces were stronger and they would ravage the conquered cities of all they possessed. The men, women and children were not spared even when they surrendered.

Brenda and her people watched this happen and could not tolerate the savageness of it all. The Assembly was in an uproar and demanded that they put a stop to King Barborda's reign. Mounting a powerful force of air and land units they went out to try to put a stop to this carnage. Once King Barborda's army seen them coming they quickly turned around and retreated back to their homeland. The survivors were then brought back to Tarmish and many taken to the hospitals.

There were other skirmishes around the world with the other nations and a couple did make peace but not all of them. Things did settle down and King Barborda's people moved further south where fruits and vegetables grew naturally. This was a blessing and a curse in that they didn't need to learn how to grow them only just to plant and ration the food. The curse was he went on to build a very large and powerful military so whenever he would notice that a weaker neighbor would have something he wanted he would simply attack them and take it.

Even though this was far away from Tarmish the people there were not oblivious to his deeds. Brenda would then quickly send an air strike to cut off his supply lines so he couldn't advance just retreat. Barborda's army didn't conquer they just attacked with force to kill and then loot, this was very much like the Barbarians of the old Earth.

The nations of Sorentito left their northern homes and moved south to where King Barborda was. This left only a small nation in South America that had already joined the *Tres Vagans* and the one very violent one in North America. The Sorentito's of North America were more powerful that the ones belonging to King Barborda. They had attacked and conquered the Tres Vagan nation there hundreds of years ago. Even though they were very much a military people they did allow the Tres Vagans to farm and realizing the benefit of this they gave them some basic freedoms.

The people of Tarmish would travel the world and visit their relatives in the other free nations. Life was good so they continued building schools, hospitals and had plenty of sport games for enjoyment. Since the first meeting of the leaders on Machu Picchu, many hundreds of years ago, and what they learned there from Master Herthro about conscious control. They soon created a school for people with the power of conscious thought. It produced many Masters that would direct and control through their minds the outcome of many battles.

Finally the day had come when the lack of interest of Masters had become less. There were very few wars and only one or two Masters would come out and control it until the day that the military technology was so great that it was enough to defeat the enemy. Master Herthro was growing old and he didn't possess the power he once had. The people of Tarmish and the other nations became very complacent about these ideas. Only play, making money and some weird religions were what interested them.

There was a small group of Tres Vagans that still believed in the ancient teachings of the High Councilor Brenda and could see the destructive path the people were on. They tried to teach and warn them but in doing so it only made them mad. Soon their anger was so great that the followers of High Councilor Brenda left the city with her to escape their new laws banning the old ways. Brenda learned of a coup in the Assembly and determined that she did not possess the numbers to stop this so she quietly left with her people.

Leaving the city of Tarmish for good was a very sad day. They moved north northeast to a very cold and desolate area with a sea that was frozen six months out of the year. There they were free to continue the Masters school, and to invent many things that would create a near perfect civilization. But mostly their main mission was peace through deep meditation.

Brenda and Brad were getting very old and their children are now grandparents too. They had two grandsons from their daughter and one of them was married and had a daughter. As she reflected on her life she thought about plight of these Master Vagans.

Reverence

Teaching us they were here to do.
Finding a way they helped us live.
By their example we could see this.
The Masters gave us all their bliss.

One conquers body, mind and word.
In what you do, think and are heard.

They are Masters in the game of life.
Honor them for they are worthy.
Or as the flower, they fade away.
Gone is the knowledge of the way.

One conquers body, mind and word.
In what you do, think and are heard

CHAPTER 10

Daisy's father had fought in the last war when she was just a baby. Then there was peace for many years and she grew up on the beach surfing along with her twin brothers. Life was good there. In high school she was involved in sports and government. Her parents were so proud of her.

On a very hot day when she was a junior the AC went out in the high school. The teachers opened the doors and windows but there wasn't any breeze. So the students were getting rowdy and some started to fight. Daisy was her class president and when she caught word of the fighting she went into action.

Walking very calmly with her two assistants to where the ruckus was they arrived just outside of the danger area and she motioned for her two assistants to stop. Very quietly she said to them let's form in a circle and meditate for a resolution to this conflict. The fight was raging and in the distance, the principle was coming with the football coach, and some of the team to put an end to it forcibly.

Before they could arrive Daisy and her entourage finished their meditation and stood up. Daisy started walking toward the fight and her two assistants were just a few feet behind her. With her hands held in front of her in a peaceful way this caused some in the fight to notice her as she kept walking toward them. The fight started to become less and less intense and as she entered right in the middle her assistants joined her. They stood facing the fighters in each of three directions roughly 120 degrees apart.

From a distance the principle saw them in the middle and was ready to call on the coach to send his players in. He quickly felt the need to do this to prevent the three in the middle from getting hurt. That was until he noticed that the fighting had all be ceased shortly after this. Holding his hand back touching the coach's shoulder he said "I believe Daisy has this under control."

That was one of the many things she did growing up in *Otium,* the city that Brenda's people started after leaving Tarmish many years ago. She went on to graduate with honors, and was voted as the class president each year. In sports she excelled too and received scholarships in volleyball, tennis and golf. Picking what university to go to wouldn't be that easy and in this she will get some help.

Wanting to go to the same school as her boyfriend of many years was going to be tricky. He was set on medical school and she wanted to learn government and talking tonight they both decided that they would just have to see each other after school. Daisy then got a call from her grandmother and heard her say "dear I'm coming over this week end to visit. I would like to talk with you about school."

"Okay grandma I'll see you then."

Their life on Millennia hasn't been completely uneventful but mostly they spent the time trying to improve things. Tamla and Shasha were involved in spying on Brenda from time to time when their curiosity would pique. There was always for them the mode of astral travel and these girls were experts at it.

Tonight they would travel and visit Brenda and observe her talking with her granddaughter about college.

Brenda was a master in meditation and she taught her children and her grandchildren this. Tonight she spent longer than normal because the further she went inside the more comfortable she felt. Waking up she then sat and wondered where those thoughts and feelings were from. This really captivated her heart and mind to the point that after turning in for bed she reached out... and said "I don't know who you are but I've felt your presence for a very long time. If you are gods or angels it doesn't matter to me. I am not afraid to meet you. So please contact me if you will, I do want your presence to be known"

Tamla and Shasha were right there in her room with her once she made that statement of wanting contact. They now have their reason to contact her but the question now was, where are they going to take her? Shasha looked at Tamla, then smiled, and said "let's take her to the High Council. Mom would love to see her there again."

"That might just work we are always in need of wisdom from her Grace."

That pillow was just what she needed when her head hit it. Brad could tell see was in deep thought, and that there was something bothering her, so he was content with only a kiss goodnight. As she thought about the meditation she had before and how this feeling seemed to engulf her, she became more and more tired. Then slipping into a deep sleep, her mind would stop thinking about the day, and just quietly float into a cosmic stream of bliss.

While dreaming she could see these two figures coming toward her. Not scared or even that curious she seemed to know them but not by name. Waiting until they came closer she could then see their faces and said "I seem to know both of you but I can't remember where or what your names are."

Tamla answered and said "that's because your memory has been restarted and the ones you have of the three planets are not real."

Speechless for what seemed like all night Brenda finally spoke and when she did she tripped on her words. "You, you, you mean I'm not real?"

Laughing and fighting the urge not to tell her too much Shasha said "we will take you to some places in your sleep and I'm sure it will all come back to you."

"Okay then I won't ask too many questions so you won't need to tell me too many lies." She then looked at them both and grinned.

Tamla put her hand up and said "whoa, whoa we aren't lying to you."

"Then what do you call my three planet memories?"

Shasha said "touché"

They spent a couple of hours briefly telling her some things to prepare her for their next planned visit to the High Council. The thought was that if they took her there cold then she would bog Daanic down with useless questions. So off they went and Brenda found that she really enjoyed astral travel.

After they landed on the High Council, Brenda asked Shasha "so this is the place? It appears to be part of the Pleaides right?"

Tamla went over to her and said "daughter you get a prize."

"That's what I thought it was but it was merely a guess."

Shasha wanted to tell her that she was their daughter but thought that she would ask Daanic first. Visiting the High Council for the first time made Brenda feel very fortunate and she let them know just that. Ringo was there and Tamla introduced her to him then Brenda shook his hand and said "you look familiar and so is your name."

"Well that's because I might have been named after a drummer in an iconic band from the former Earth?"

"Former Earth, what are you talking about?"

Tamla grabbed his hand and said "careful what you say Ringo."

"Oh sorry about that I'll be more careful next time."

The room started to become noisy as the chiefs and elders started to enter. Brenda stood and looked around just amazed at how many there were and that their outfits seemed so unassumingly plain. Not that she was unimpressed it was just that she expected them to be more flamboyant. As they took their seats the room was now quiet and Leto's voice boomed "all stand in honor of our High Councilor her Grace Daanic."

The two large doors opened and there she walked in with her entourage. Beautiful just beautiful Brenda said to her two hostesses. Moving gracefully down the aisle Daanic had fixed her eyes on Brenda. This did make her a little uncomfortable and as Daanic approached her and stopped she seemed to hold her breath! Then the High Councilor put her hands on her shoulders and said "my dear granddaughter how have you been. Oh we know how you've been…"

Tamla said "oh mom, there you go again with your old classic rock lyrics. Well, welcome to the machine is not what we have here."

Brenda gathered herself and said "Your Grace did you call me your granddaughter?"

"Yes I did sweetie, I sure did, and it's time you know who you really are."

Shasha hugged Daanic and said "thanks mom we've wanted to tell her that."

Then she turned and finished her walk to the podium and sat down as the council took over. Then the whole council spent the rest of the evening showing Brenda hologram movies of her prior life on Earth and Millennia. Filled with a universal heritage that she never knew she had, but she did feel there was something more that she didn't know.

After the girls left the council Daanic felt the need to write another song.

My Life

Never knowing who you are
Until that day you see
Finding Love in someone
And there you'll be

Your Spirit flies like a dove
In this energy that's meant to be
Knowing all is pure Love

You need Love and Love needs you
You need Love and Love will find

The magic in your heart and mind

Drown in fear and hate is not wise
Drop the stone that drags you down
Learn to Love and witness the prize

In this universe you are many things
Living, loving, learning and seeing
A peaceful heart is what Loves brings
Only hope and faith are your being

You need Love and Love needs you
You need Love and Love will find
The magic in your heart and mind

Nothing is lost from life to life
All that's learned is stored within
Love, hate, ease and even strife
Become a tapestry ready to begin

You build a Spirit that embraces
People are not easy to remember
But their Spirit is in small traces

You need Love and Love needs you
You need Love and Love will find
The magic in your heart and mind

It's always good to get a song from Daanic (Margo) and now that Brenda has started writing songs it appears that tradition continues. Who knows maybe Shasha or Tamla will be next?

Brenda awoke, looked to see if Brad was in bed and he wasn't because just like the roosters he can't sleep when the sun rises. So then mumbling she said "guess I need to go out and find him."

Out of the bed to the bathroom then dressed and downstairs for a cup of the tea he made. The aroma penetrated upstairs and her taste buds begged her to get downstairs and pour a cup. "Yum" she says, as the door opens, and she goes in search of Brad.

Walking through the barn she's searching and thinking about her dream while noticing that Brad is nowhere to be found. Not sure how she will tell him about her dream, but one thing is that she remembers it very well. Looking over at the tractor and he's not there she proceeds to the new field of watermelons he planted this week. Still no Brad and she's now getting anxious and wanting so much to talk with him.

Turning the corner around the trees she spots him relaxing over by the lake. Sleeping in a hammock of all things, thinking about dumping him out of it she stops that thought, smiles and says to herself "he doesn't deserve that, but it would be fun." Walking over to him she leans over, gives him a kiss, and says "wake up my prince I have something to share with you."

Stretching and yawning he says "oh I guess I need to wake up then."

"Yes you do, I had a dream last night..."

"Okay you had a dream that's what you need to tell me?"

Realizing that he wasn't quite awake yet she just smiled at him and waited.

Brad then said "I'm awake now tell me about this dream."

"Before I went to sleep I was in meditation and I felt a presence there that I thought I knew. It seemed to get stronger and stronger so that my senses were really alert." Taking a sip of tea, and a deep breath she went on to say "I then asked this Spirit that if it wanted to contact me then I'm not afraid and I welcomed that."

She paused for a minute and Brad said "is that all that happened, so where does this dream come in?"

"No, when I went to sleep I meet two women, one named Shasha, and the other was Tamla." They just introduced themselves in name only and said I knew them before on a planet called Millennia?"

He was then hanging on her every word and said "that name sounds familiar."

"I know they then told me some information about how I knew them and that we are going to meet someone I knew before." Closing her eyes and then hugging herself she told him the rest of the story "I was brought to a place called the High Council and it was in the Pleaides star system. There I meet the High Councilor Daanic. When she walked up to me, she put her hands on my shoulders, and said "how are you doing my granddaughter?"

He almost choked and said "granddaughter, High Councilor, and the Pleaides? You sure do dream big!"

"Laugh all you want but they sure knew a lot and I was told I would visit again. By the way Shasha and Tamla are my moms or parents if you prefer."

Brenda was given information that no one has been privileged to know. Most people would probably just go crazy if they even believed it. However she would visit with her moms again and see grandma once in a while.

CHAPTER 11

Born in Tarmish she was very young when her daddy went to war. Mom had told her that he was a hero and he died saving the lives of others. When he was conscripted he had just finished his medical training and was going to do his residency. The Army made him a doctor and shipped him to the front.

Tarmish was against fighting but after being bombed from the Sorentito's many times they decided that this would need to stop. War was declared by the Assembly and a series of attacks were carried out on the enemy's current positions. The Assembly did draw the line at not attacking the civilian populations.

Although Tarmish was very successful in that they did eventually drive the enemy back to their homeland. However they did suffer some devastating bombings on their headquarters, which also included the hospitals, and that's where her daddy died in the operating room trying to save lives.

This was a time when the Tres Vagans had all but lost their desire to meditate and to train their people to become masters of thought and how to control the situations around them. The few masters that were left decided to leave and Daisy went with Brenda and the rest of their family.

Here we are years later and Daisy has finished high school. She is ready to attend college and learn politics. Her boyfriend Rick is studying to become a doctor and today they are having lunch together. Rick said to her "I'm really swamped with these classes I have to take. I didn't realize medical school would be so hard."

She knew that he wanted to be a doctor since they met in seventh grade. Holding his hand tightly she released it and then placed her head on his shoulder. Looking up into his blue eyes she said "yes but you are smart and determined to be a doctor."

"Are you using your Master Vagan mind tricks on me?" He said with one eyebrow up.

"I have always used my mind powers to control you. Do you not like the way you've turned out so far?"

His eyes got big, his lips pursed tight, and he then said "wow I believe you have been doing that, at least since high school." He then stood up and took her hand and said "walk with me I want to look at the water in the pond with you and see the ripples at the same time you do."

"You are so romantic I wonder where you get that from."

A wonderful lunch spent with the one you have given your heart to for all these years and knowing that you still have a whole lifetime ahead. This thought sure was on their minds as they looked at the ripples in the water created by the swans.

Back to school they both had to part and go their separate ways. Daisy thought what if she indeed was controlling Rick in some way all these years? Contemplating on this she concluded with a resounding "hell yes" I've been doing that and he has turned out pretty good so far!

There in her civics class she was very happy, civilian government had always appealed to her, and over the last several years she had spent many hours with her grandma Brenda. Today the professor was lecturing on social programs and he was a little too liberal for Daisy's liking. Not that she didn't like him, she did! He was very knowledgeable and pleasant to talk with.

Daisy's civics' professor raved on and on about how we should take money from the wealthy to give to the poor. She didn't totally disagree but she often wondered when and why doesn't it end? She studied the whole system and found that it did seem to create a pattern of dependency. Not only did Daisy learn from her grandma about civil government, but she also spent time with her Grandpa Brad working on a farm tractor.

As a little girl going to visit her daddy's parents on the farm was such an amazing treat. Not that it was full of play it wasn't at all. In fact she would work with grandpa, plowing, planting and watering the fields. Then relax in the evening with grandma discussing politics and mostly learning about civil government. The times of elections to share the results with grandma or when the harvest was ready, and grandpa needed her help. These were memories that she would always go back to.

Getting back to the lecture she put all that learning to good use. Knowing that she is a Vagan Master she has been asked not to try and influence anyone unless it's to prevent problems. Listening and taking notes while she also put together some ideas in class.

One time when her Professor seemed to tire out, she asked this question "Professor won't all the people be better served if we didn't talk about taking from the rich and giving to the poor?" She didn't want to push the subject too far. She learned that it's better to just get the dialog started and then slowly give your ideas or points.

'Well Ms. Cole I suppose that is something that could be looked into. Are you saying that I do not mention the *redistribution of wealth* because it is a touchy subject?"

"I don't know if *touchy* is the way I would put it." Stopping right there is hard to do but it is important. Going further could only cause the other person to feel overwhelmed with your information.

"Okay, then how would you describe it?" Notice that he is not offering any suggestions or giving his thoughts of solving the problem.

"Thanks for asking. What I've been taught in communicating with all types of people is that first you must understand where they are coming from." Another pause and she noticed that he seemed to like what she said.

The other students always looked forward to when these two would debate civil policies. The Professor would benefit because this would stimulate the class and they would receive high marks. Noticing the time he then said "another time "Ms. Cole I look forward to exchanging meaningful words with you again." There will be plenty more times that these two will work out the civil government issues in the classroom.

After school some of her friends in the political majors would hang out at one of the local pubs. The special thing about this pub was that instead of being big and popular it was upstairs, small and quiet. It was called Plotinus' Pub, it was named after a great philosopher of the planet Fyrooth, but was really from Greece of the 3rd century previous Earth age. Note I said "some of her friends" that means the majority of the political majors would meet elsewhere somewhere big and loud.

At the Plotinus' Pub they could speak softly and discuss issues rationally. Another important thing was that most of these students are Vagan Masters while the others are friends who just like no drama. The owner goes way back in time to before they arrived on the new Earth. Her name is Gloria, and even though she never was on a planet called Hydrumn, she was from Millennia, and knew Brenda there. Here she is a Vagan Master in the mold of an Obi-Wan Kenobi.

Tonight they were discussing the pending vote in the Assembly to help their impoverished people of Tarmish. This has been in the works for many years while Otium has helped them out with food and military support. This bill now has more lasting conditions than just to help them with their material needs. It's briefly written to suggest that Tarmish become a less hostile people and seek guidance on how to prosper without destroying their environment.

She could only stay for one or maybe two glasses of wine until she had to leave and meet Rick for dinner. There were no arguments and most of them talked while they played a form of a chess game. The main disagreement was that if they were going to use the assistance they gave to Tarmish as a means of correcting their ways then why not just annex them? Some thought that this would be disastrous because then they would have unrestricted entry into Otium and it would then be destroyed. Here they learned that all of their decisions do have their own set of consequences.

They have talked about marriage many times and they've always come to the same conclusions. They both agreed that it would be better to wait until they finished with college. At least their first four years because Daisy would eventually say "I'm not waiting some eight years for you to finish med school."

He didn't say it enough for her liking, but he loved her very much, and she knew that they would marry one day. Tonight he wanted to talk about school and something he learned in Quantum Biology. Waiting for her to arrive he sat and thought about how exciting that class was. Going over and over in his mind what he learned in class until out of the corner of his eye he spotted his lovely Daisy. Standing up he then walked over to her, sat her down and then gave her a kiss.

"Why do you look so excited?" Daisy asked.

'In my Quantum Biology class today I learned something very cool." He then took a sip of wine and sat back smiling.

"Well what did you learn?"

"I learned about how you can change the shape of water just by different vibrations."

Daisy didn't want to suppress his excitement so she said "Okay what are the shapes?"

'Well it all depends on the vibrations of the music or the words spoken."

He went on to elaborate on how positive words create beautiful images and hateful words create disturbing shapes. She was fascinated about this and he shared with her how he wasn't sure if he was going to become a surgeon or a physicist. She wasn't too sure about politics either because she was enjoying learning about philosophy very much. Knowing that like her he was a freshman and they both will change their minds in the next couple of years he felt they were certainly on the right track.

After dinner their conversation turned to politics and she learned that they do have some different opinions.

Looking at her empty water glass she said "what do you think about our new bill to help Tarmish?"

"Well I haven't really read much of it, but it sounds good from what I know." Pouring her some more water he then put down the carafe and brought his hands together.

This man, who will one day be her husband and a doctor of some type of medicine, was looking so innocent that she had to be gentile with him. With a very small chuckle she said "true from what little they have released it does seem to be a good idea."

"But?" he said while avoiding her eyes and looking at the dessert menu.

Before she noticed the dessert menu she said "let me study it some more before I render my complete ruling on it." Then she noticing him flash the menu said "no dessert tonight I believe I've had too much wine to introduce sugar into my system."

"Okay my Love then let's leave this place. I'll drive you home."

Days and days pass and school is becoming more and more exciting for these two young lovers. The bill to help Tarmish passed both houses of the Assembly and Brenda signed it after making a few changes that were confirmed by both houses. She didn't like this provision that Tarmish wasn't annexed and they were given more freedom to roam inside Otium. Daisy didn't either and she came up with a solution.

Visiting her grandma and talking about this bill and how to make it better. They talked about how the streets of Otium were becoming filled with people from Tarmish just hanging around begging for money. Brenda was a kind soul and so was Daisy but they didn't see any reason to have their city destroyed by people who for many years rejected knowledge.

Daisy started their conversation with "how are the plans to educate our fellow Tres Vagans from Tarmish coming along."

"I think you know the answer to that one. They have rejected our attempts to do that and even when they show up for the mandatory classes they don't want to learn."

"I guess it's a quagmire then?"

"It does seem that way. How are your studies at the university coming along?"

'Fine, I have a professor in civics that likes to debate with me in class, and he's very liberal even more so than myself. After school my friends and I hang out at this pub, where the proprietor's name is Gloria, and she is a long time Vagan Master. I like to talk things out with her a few nights a week. Plus she makes a killer pumpkin cream pie."

"Sounds great I do hope the universities aren't disturbed too much with our influx of new citizens. Now tell me what your idea of improving the bill is?"

"Well I was thinking that we need to use a form of mind control on the ones that are here."

"That's a good idea except we don't really have that many Vegan Masters anymore."

"Grandma I can probably get several for you to complete their training."

Being very pleased with her granddaughter's steadfastness and willingness to join in and help. Brenda said "my dear I will take you up on that" and she then opened up her glass tablet and looked at her schedule. After closing the tablet she then said "meet me in four days at the Assembly at fourteen hundred hours." Hugs were exchanged and they both turned in for the night.

Waiting for her in bed, Brad asked "how was your time with Daisy tonight?"

"It was great! She will be a wonderful leader one day. That's if she chooses to be in politics."

"Well I believe she would be a very caring and successful farmer if she wanted to. The way Daisy carefully tills the ground and creates the schedule for the yearly planning for the crop rotations. She also knows when to plant or when to let a field stay dormant for a season. Very careful consideration for the ground and the environment we need more farmers like her."

They both kissed and maybe did something else that won't be mentioned here. Let's just say they both woke up with big smiles on their faces.

Brenda awoke early with Brad and followed him downstairs for some tea and scones. Then outside to the lake where she went to write this song about her granddaughter Daisy and her love for Rick.

A Forever Love

Forged in the shadows of grief
Love we share won't be brief
Knowing that our Love will live
Stronger in all that I have to give

Love is forever, a forever Love
Find this wherever you are
Love is forever, a forever Love
Inside your Heart find your star

Love is young no matter when

A heart is always ready to begin
Go down the river and don't fight
Travelling to a place in the light

Love is forever, a forever Love
Find this wherever you are
Love is forever, a forever Love
Inside your Heart find your star

Talking and listening is the key
Become one with your Love to be
Doing this is the only path of one
An eternal life forever to be won

Love is forever, a forever Love
Find this wherever you are
Love is forever, a forever Love
Inside your Heart find your star

She later gave this to Daisy before she left and it made her cry with tears of joy. Four days later she brought eight of her friends from school that she knew from Plotinus' Pub. She even managed to bring Gloria with her too and at the steps of the Assembly they were waiting to see Brenda.

Brenda was summoned and instead of sending someone to bring them in she did it herself. Seeing Daisy from afar she started to increase her step and her aide had trouble keeping up. Nearly out of breath she said "Daisy my dear, I see you brought your friends today."

"Yes I did, grandma, and I even brought Gloria the Vagan Master I told you about."

Brenda and Gloria looked at each other and then Brenda said "I remember you when we were building the ships. Aren't you from Hydrumn?"

"Why yes I am Your Grace and we worked together to convince my people to join the others in preparing to leave the planets."

"I think I remember some of that. I did meet with a lot of people. Well let's get inside we have a lot of work to do"

They followed her and then she laid out a plan to teach them with Gloria's help into becoming Vagan Masters. This took some time, since they were still involved with teaching the new citizens. Some were formed into teams, and sent to Tarmish, a few times a week to teach them.

Progress was being made even though there was a lot of resistance. Crime increased in Otium and decreased in Tarmish while this was certainly both good and bad news. Daisy would still have some intense discussions with her civics professor and he believed that more should be done to help the people of Tarmish even at the determent to their city.

CHAPTER 12

Trying and trying to bring them along are the Vagan Masters. Gloria took the lead and her students are giving it all they can. Only one class in Tarmish was started to help the people that didn't travel to Otium. Tonight Daisy traveled there with another one of her fellow masters. She is teaching them about farming by showing them how to properly care for their land.

With her friend Julie from the school and the pub they are feeling that these people don't want to learn. One of the students asked them "so why should we care about taking care of the land. All we really want to do is farm it and take the food it delivers."

Julie answered his question by citing "when we love the land the land will love us back, now why is this so hard to understand?"

"It's hard to understand because we are the lords of this Earth."

Seeing that most if not all of the class was in agreement with this statement they both weren't sure what to say next. Then Daisy who understood that this was becoming an argument that wouldn't end well decided to say this "Okay, I see your point and yes we are the lords of this planet." She thought it was better to agree and make peace than let a problem escalate further.

Wanting to say something else Julie could see what Daisy was doing, so she decided that it would be better to just bring the class to an end. With this knowledge she said "we need to end class tonight, thank you all for coming."

On the ride back to Otium they both had a long conversation on the direction this class is going. "Well that sure was a close call" Daisy spoke after several minutes of silence.

"Close call, you did the right thing by agreeing with him."

"Thanks, now how do you suppose we can turn around their way of thinking?"

"Daisy your guess is as good as mine. It seems that they aren't swayed or even affected by our mind powers."

"I know and I wonder if we can even be of help to them? It seems that they have gone so far in the direction of hate and selfishness that there might not be a return back for them."

"Maybe we can discuss this with Gloria and see what she thinks?"

"Hum I think that's a great idea." Daisy then pulled over into a local coffee shop just inside of town and said "want some coffee?"

"Sounds great maybe some pie too!"

Laughing she grabbed her hand and said "are you using your mind power on me? Well it is working."

The coffee was perfect, hot and blended with some cream. The pie was apple or cherry and they both choose the opposite. Enjoying each other's company, especially after their close call in Tarmish, Daisy said "I think I have a solution to our current problem."

"Okay then, tell me what your solution is because I'm all ears right now."

"Okay let's not tell Gloria about the problem yet..."

"But we are required to give a report on our status."

"I know but shouldn't we try and resolve it before burdening her? I mean she has three other groups reporting problems."

Julie was excited and said "then, let's give her a report that only mentions some problems we have, but nothing we can't handle. Now what is this solution I'm sure it's just not reporting the problems to Gloria?"

"You will go with me to visit my grandma Brenda this week end..."

"You mean the High Councilor? I've never met her in person before, what should I wear and how am I to act around her..."

Grabbing her hands and telling her "calm down Julie you will be my guest and we will be at her farm where it is very laid back."

"Okay I like this idea because I feel that she will know how to solve this problem."

This evening they both talked about problems and solutions. As Vagan Masters they were more and more understanding of how important it is to have an open mind in this world. Daisy would make the call as soon as they left and were driving home.

Brenda was happy to hear from her and although reporting to Gloria is the right thing to do. She was impressed with her granddaughter's way of accessing a problem and coming up with ways to find the solutions. She told her "baby you did the right thing coming to me. I would like for you to include Gloria so give her an invite from me to attend."

"Okay grandma you are so wise to do this. Love you and we'll see you then."

Brenda could hear Julie in the car and said "what's your friend's name?"

"It's Julie, she and I are teaching in Tarmish together."

"Well okay I look forward to seeing you this week end Julie."

A sense of warmth came over her and she wasn't sure she could answer so she could only say "thank you Your Grace."

During the week Julie was thinking about her visit with the High Councilor. When she was in class with Daisy she couldn't wait to ask questions about her grandma. They did however have another class and even though they were on a rotation they both volunteered to go back to Tarmish.

In their class tonight they knew what to expect and were on their toes. Even when some in the classroom would try and provoke them into an argument the girls were wise enough to either agree or change the subject. That is if they could do it peacefully, they had the promise of knowing that they would meet with Brenda in just two days, and this gave them the courage to make it through.

Showing up at grandma's this week end with her Vagan Master teacher Gloria, Daisy brought her friend and teaching companion Julie. Walking out to meet her was grandpa and he knew she wasn't there to help him on the farm. He did hope to get her and her friends out there a little to see some of the pumpkins she helped him plant that were starting to bloom.

"Hello grandpa how are you doing?"

"I'm fine, your pumpkins are coming along very well, do you want to see them later?"

"Yes I do, but it's too late now so let's see them in the morning."

Going inside and finding their rooms, their guests took a few minutes to get settled in and then Brenda sent Daisy up to bring them down for dinner. Nothing like home cooked meals and in Brenda's former life (one that she's recently been told about) one of her moms was an excellent French chef and still is.

Ah, Brenda's cooking is exquisite and all were enjoying the taste. Gloria said that it brought back some very old memories. Brad was enjoying all the company, he assisted Brenda in any way he could and he poured them some wine that he made right there on the farm.

Dinner really hit the spot and the girls made their way into the study. Brad went along to listen and maybe even add some non-political advice. This was certainly not unwelcomed in fact both Gloria and Brenda suggested it.

Brenda started off their conversation by announcing "tonight I would like to only hear the problems that you are having and then tomorrow we will discuss the options of correcting them."

Gloria spoke up and said "okay who wants to go first?"

Daisy looked over at Julie and nodded for her to start.

Julie then said "we are being challenged by the students in Tarmish on anything we try to teach them."

Brenda said "Daisy do you have anything to add?"

"Yes, I do. Not only are they challenging us they are borderline on edging toward violence."

This didn't sit well with Brenda or Gloria and Brad certainly didn't like it either but the first night he didn't want to say anything until all the information was devolved. It was getting late and Brenda suggested some chamomile tea with some meditation before turning in.

Tonight Brenda travelled again with her two guides that just happened to be her moms too. "Well it looks like I'm back with my family tonight" she said as Tamla and Shasha showed up in her dream.

"Why yes you are my dear, we are going to have some visitors tonight" Tamla told her as Shasha welcomed her with a hug.

"Thanks mom I really needed the hug and who are our new visitors going to be?"

"Dear, you met your grandmother Daanic the High Councilor of the Pleiades. Well, her mother will be here, and her mother's mother too, now isn't that confusing?"

Then Shasha said "wait until you see what they are."

Brenda then gasped and said "what they are?'

Before you could say the seven stars of the Pleiades they showed up. Flying in a large purplish cloud just formed and then a bright blast appeared followed by some loud thunder. The cloud broke and three dragons appeared, one of them was white and the other two black. The white one spoke and said "hello Brenda my name is Jillela and I am your great grandma from the old Earth."

She stood there mesmerized and said "but you are a dragon and a beautiful one at that! So how can we be related?"

"My dear we are not these bodies, we are in fact all Spirits from the Source."

"Well, okay I guess so. I haven't really learned that yet."

"You will my dear, you certainly will."

Putting her in between her and Shasha, Tamla said "grandma where is Ella is she coming?"

"Yes she is, she was taking care of some new planets being formed in another galaxy. I'm sure she'll be here soon."

Trying to take this all in Brenda started to feel overwhelmed. What with learning that her great grandmother is a dragon. Now to hear that her great-grandmother is taking care of some new planets that are being formed in another galaxy is even more to contemplate. So after processing this, she then asked "so what is she, a star?"

Smiling Jillela said "well not yet but one day I'm sure. We all will go back to that eventually."

Flying in was an alicorn and Brenda just loved unicorns, alicorns, and Pegasus's too. This made her excited that she even jumped up and down. She had never seen one in person only in movies and pictures. After coming in for a landing this alicorn then walked right up to Brenda and said "you don't remember me do you?"

"Nope I can't say that I do as a matter of fact I don't know any alicorns."

"Well my name is Ella and I was the High Councilor before Jillela and Daanic were."

Tamla said "okay enough with the introductions let's talk about Brenda's needs on Earth. Her granddaughter is dealing with some trouble makers and we need to give her some universal advice."

Daanic said "then let's get started."

The rest of the evening was spent going over what Daisy and Julie had told Brenda. All of her family talked and discussed how this needed to be handled and Brenda was somewhat surprised by some of the advice she was given.

The next morning when she awoke, it was early, and Brad was still in bed, so she waited for him to wake up. It wasn't that long and while she waited she went over the information in her head. When he awoke she said "good morning, my husband guess where I was last night?"

"I'm going to say the Pleiadian High Council."

"Nope just on Millennia with my two moms, my grandma, great-grandma and my great-great-grandma."

"Wow now that's a family reunion."

She went on to explain to him her dream and all the advice she was given. Now she needed to get dressed and head downstairs to start her day, for she had guests to wait on. She tackled Brad when he came out of the closet while he held the clothes that he was going to wear this day. On the bed they were, he had an idea, but she quickly squashed it!

"Brad you make the tea and I'll put together some fruit and cereal for our guests. I don't want them to feel too stuffed and fruit always keeps me sharp."

"Okay then, on my way downstairs and I'll help you with the fruit. You know, I brought some fresh melons in yesterday."

Waking up to the wonderful smell of a jasmine mint tea that filled the upstairs it's this aroma. Brenda could hear them stirring in their rooms. Brad smiled at her and said "works every time it's tried."

"Yes it does. Now let's get ready to serve them!"

A plethora of good mornings went all around the table until Brenda said with a big wink "enough we need to eat our breakfast and get real serious."

Daisy said "grandma you seem to be in good Spirits this morning. Does that mean you have the answers we need?"

Not being told that she can share her dreams with anyone outside of Brad. This made it a little difficult to explain without lying, so she answered in the only way she could by putting her hands across her heart, and saying "I was visited by angels last night and they gave me the answers." Well put, and breakfast was enjoyed.

Their meeting can now begin and today Brad will be a participant as well. To start the meeting off Brenda asked that they all observe some time for deep meditation to release all unwanted energy. Breathing in deep with the sounds of water flowing and some soft chanting music they were releasing stress, worry, and anxiety. The small group in this room then opened their eyes and noticed that there was an energy that one could feel in their hearts. Coming back to their purpose of being in this meeting the group looked at Brenda and all nodded that they were ready to begin discussions. With their blessings she then sang this song that she wrote early in the morning;

Master's Wisdom

Words you say flow around
Give of yourself understand all
Hear this magnificent sound

Teaching is your call to the masses
Worlds of information you teach
Care for them while in your classes

A Master's Wisdom for the call
This wisdom is given to us all
Wisdom to learn to live in Love
Perfect fit like a hand in a glove

See blue and see white in the sky
Things can change with the wind
It will be dark you wonder why

None are exempt from change
Look at both find what's common
Left then right opinions arrange

A Master's Wisdom for the call
This wisdom is given to us all
Wisdom to learn to live in Love
Perfect fit like a hand in a glove

Build on good things to share
Move your heart in this direction
Don't resist or watch and stare

All wrongs need to be stopped
Down the river of eternal peace
The fuse just has to be chopped

A Master's Wisdom for the call
This wisdom is given to us all
Wisdom to learn to live in Love
Perfect fit like a hand in a glove

CHAPTER 13

Brenda's song was a great help for the girls and in Tarmish many people were helped by the teachings of these young Vagan Masters. Times were good and the Masters temple flourished in Tarmish for a time, but the people of Sorentito continued to build war machines and ignore good farming practices. In time the Sorentito people had become more and more a barbaric type of society and King Barborda ruled them with an iron fist.

As it was meant to be the day had come where King Barborda's rule brought Sorentito to a great desperation for food and supplies. With only a military and nothing else to bargain with they attacked Tarmish with all they had. Knowing that Tarmish was a city of peaceful people and not prepared for this large of an attack. Otium didn't see this coming and couldn't supply reinforcements fast enough.

Many weeks passed and Tarmish was surrounded by these desperate people. Brenda met with her top advisor Herthro to devise a rescue plan. Her granddaughter Daisy was trapped in there with Julie her friend. Knowing this wouldn't be easy the people of Otium did have one thing going for them. Their city was north in the ice and snow on a mountain range and nearly impenetrable on many sides.

The Vagan Masters could not use their powers on their own people but the enemy was another story. The plan that was made consisted of three groups and they put them together on their way to Tarmish. The night was very dark and full of clouds with no moon out tonight. With extensive knowledge of the city, the plan took shape very quickly, and the teams are on their way to rescue Daisy, Julie, and as many others as they can.

Approaching the city the teams split up and went in different directions. They were formed as one main team to do the rescue, the second one to create a diversion, and the third to provide cover for the first one when they make their exit out. On the east side, team two was in position, and prepared to create a distraction. While team three cased the back gate and recorded the times that the enemy would post their new guards. Then team one took a high position near the back gate where they could observe the third team's progress.

It was communicated out that the enemy would post new guards every four hours and that those guards would rotate every third shift. As the first shift made their shift change team three used their mind power to lure them out to be captured. Then team three changed into their uniforms and put prison ones on the enemy. Four hours passed and when the second shift showed up they were taken over by the masters and also put into prison clothes. After the third shift is captured that's when they could start the next phase.

The second team was ready to start their diversion and now the time was right. Then team one rushed into the city, where they went there was a celebration started by the people, because of their arrival to free them. They then quickly instructed them to be quiet because they didn't want the enemy to become alert to what they were doing. The night was getting old and there were only a couple of hours left before the sun would start to show. Knowing this they made haste and found Daisy and Julie with several other people and they were instructed not to turn back to try to get anyone else if they wanted to escape now.

Under the cover of the night the lights at the back gate were turned off. Then team three opened the gates and team one then passed by. Now the third team dressed in the enemy's clothes went inside and had supplies brought in for the people. Once the signal was given, they were on their way back to Otium, and then team two would create another diversion.

Tarmish was happy to receive the supplies, but didn't know when they would be rescued, and on the east side the enemy seemed to be in a celebration. When the people of Tarmish looked outside they could see that their enemy was also given supplies. Not understanding the mind of the masters they couldn't comprehend what this meant. One thing is for sure Brenda was so happy to have Daisy back.

The army of Sorentito took the supplies, returned back to their homes to share with their people, and Tarmish was free again. Now the people of Tarmish should understand what just happened, but most won't and that's a shame.

Rick was very happy to have his girl back. These few months have been very trying for him because of her travels to Tarmish and the troubles there. He didn't understand all the Vagan Master stuff but knew that Daisy has a heart of gold. With that said he wasn't going to tell her that she couldn't help people. Not when he himself was studying to be a doctor.

Today things would start to return to normal and Daisy would not be travelling to Tarmish. For some reason the people there believed that the Vagan Masters had something to do with their being seized by the Sorentito army. Gloria couldn't believe the lunacy in this; she knew that they can reject them but, it would make their agreement for help void, and what will the Assembly do about that?

Daisy and Rick wanted to just forget about these problems, and when their Spring break came, they did just that. Most of the college students either went into the mountains to ski or they would travel south to the beach. Not these two. Rick's parents had a cabin in the lowlands next to a beautiful lake. This was perfect, time alone and undisturbed with the one you love.

There they talked about their future and school. Daisy tried to leave politics out of their conversations as much as possible. Rick did talk a lot about physics, especially quantum physics. Daisy could relate to what he said, about water taking different shapes, and she thought how that relates to a Vagan Master using mind control. Before their break was over she promised her grandma that they would stop by the farm and visit for a couple of days.

"Hello grandma how are you doing?"

"Better now that you are safe. Did you know how worried poor Rick was?'

Rick said "I wasn't any more worried than your grandma and her strength helped get me through. It was terrible because I didn't know what to do to save you."

"Did you know that he begged me to let him join the rescue team? I told him no, because he didn't have the training that the Vagan Masters did, and he was very hard to say no to."

"I didn't know any of this, thanks for telling me how brave he was."

On the farm they spent two days working hard and discussing politics with grandma. Daisy showed Rick how she and her grandpa would plow the fields and plant the seeds. Knowing that Rick wasn't interested in politics Brad made sure they did something that was fun. Knowing that he was interested in physics he would show him some of the amazing techniques he would use to cause the crops to perform miracles.

Ready to go back to school they were both looking forward to nights having dinner at their favorite Italian restaurant. Wine, bread, pasta and her company is just what future doctor Rick would order. She also couldn't wait to debate her civics professor and recharge her Spiritual battery with her colleagues at Plotinus' Pub with Gloria too.

Her head on the pillow and quickly failing asleep she couldn't stay awake any longer. Brad made her as comfortable as he could because he could see the strain that the troubles in Tarmish were causing her. A feeling of despair fell all around him, he didn't understand what was happening, and when he went to sleep he found that his dreams would be invaded tonight by people he didn't think he had ever known. He asked someone in his dreams "who are you and do I know you?"

"You did at one time many years ago" said Tamla

"When and where was that?"

"You knew me on Earth before and on this planet named Millennia where you are now."

"How is that possible, I'm asleep on planet Earth?"

Shasha said "it's called dream travel or astral travel."

"Okay then what is my purpose for travelling tonight?"

Tamla and Shasha became quiet with this question. They knew what his purpose was but they wanted to bring him along slowly. Still with no answer, they went to either side of him, and held his hands. Then with a cool wind from beneath they travelled up into the sky. Gasping his breath he looked down at this beautiful planet that in his Heart he seemed to know from another life.

"Beautiful simply beautiful" he was heard to say.

Tamla spoke and said "yes we call it home, but Earth was our home at one time before now."

"Ladies, where are you taking me?"

Shasha asked Tamla "shouldn't we prepare him first?"

"Na, mom said to just bring him up."

"Okay I would never question her Grace."

"Understood, but this request came from your mom."

"Oh, I see, that's the same thing because she is her right hand."

Laughing Tamla said "yep, ever since they met at that metaphysical store in Montgomery, Alabama."

While Brad listened he couldn't help but feel that this had something to do with Brenda. Then he remembered her dream and blurted out "you two are Brenda's moms and she visited you in a dream too!"

Shasha said "give that man a prize."

"Ladies, you never answered my question. Where are you taking me?"

Then as he said that, they left Millennia's atmosphere, and Tamla shouted "into space!"

"Ha, I can see that but that's not a place because it's wet and constantly moving around. A place would be a planet or a moon."

Shasha then asked Tamla "should we tell him?"

"Sure it won't mean anything until he sees it himself."

Then gathering her thoughts Shasha said "we are taking you to the High Council of the Pleiades to meet the High Councilor."

"Well I don't remember if Brenda talked about going there. Sadly I really didn't pay much attention to what she said."

Tamla grinned and said "you'll get your chance Brad. You'll get your chance!"

Then he saw it, those seven stars, and he said "this must be it!"

Touching down and entering the council he wondered when he would awake from this dream. Not knowing what to say and certainly taking it all in was all he wanted right now. All the Chiefs were in their places, Leto up there next to the Councilor's chair while the whole scene was unreal, and somewhat magical to this farmer.

Tamla and Shasha took him to a VIP area to sit down and get ready for Leto's announcement to come. All were quiet and then the doors opened up with a soft blue light. Walking in was Daanic the High Councilor, she stopped, and Leto announced "welcome Your Grace to this assembly of your High Council of the Pleiades."

With her entourage behind her, she then walked down the aisle. Looking intently Brad couldn't believe that this was a dream because it all seemed so real. Maybe it wasn't just any ordinary dream he thought. Stepping up to the podium Daanic gracefully took the stage and her first words were "you may be seated."

Brad looked around in the area and noticed that some of the Chief's had a familiar face. His jaw dropped open and his eyes got wide when he recognized that one of them was his Brenda.

Wanting to speak to her he couldn't because he felt this unmovable force around him that seemed to prevent any speech from coming out. So he just stood there and watched her move towards the stage.

Once she was standing in front of the High Councilor and looking at her with amazement, Daanic reached out and put both of her hands on Brenda's shoulders. Watching this Brad didn't know what to think, he did feel honored, but sad at the same time. Daanic then said "welcome back home Brenda, we've missed you here."

Brad looked at Tamla and said "home! What did she mean when she said home? Her home is on Earth with me!" Then with tears streaming down his face he went on to demand "if she's staying then I'm staying too."

Tamla put her arms around him and said "we will help you and you will be able to visit her again."

"It's not the same, Daisy needs her, and I need her with me. Anyway this is just a bad dream, Brenda and I will awake from it."

Walking over to be with him, Brenda had tears too but knew that everything will work out. Coming closer to him, she said "Brad, you are going to be okay, right?"

"No I'm won't, why do you have to stay here?"

Putting her hands on her mouth, holding back a loud cry, she choked, and said "because it is meant to be, we have both been here before. After tonight your Spirit will awake and start to remember it all."

Then they both wrapped each other up and the whole council looked on. With Daanic, Jenny, Tamla and Shasha in tears as they watched their sweet Brenda say goodbye to the man she's loved in two lifetimes. The rest of the evening was spent talking about the future on Earth and how Brad will now take on a different role of support to assist Brenda with Daisy's development.

The sun was up, and in this dream he had, it seemed so real that he wasn't ready to awake. He stayed in bed past his usual time, there he thought and thought, he even prayed this "please, please just let it be a dream and I'll just lay here until she wakes me up."

Full of tears his pillow was soaked, he would move a little to see if she would stir, and still nothing, no movement at all from her. With a soft voice he said "darling are you awake?" and he heard no reply.

"Well, I guess I need to put my big boy pants on and deal with losing her." Forcing his eyes open through his many tears he said "but I don't want too!" Then to his surprise she wasn't there, quickly he thought either they took her body up or she's not dead! Up he went to the bathroom and then quickly out to throw on his clothes.

Making his way downstairs into the kitchen and then to find her still not there. His heart was beating faster and faster while his mind went through all the possible computations. All he wanted to think was that she is just somewhere on the farm. Leaving the kitchen he rushed through the house and then to her study where he still didn't locate her. Sucking in the air, breathing four times faster than normal, he took himself outside, and headed for the lake.

Turning the corner of their large thick evergreens then the lake came into view. Walking up to the gazebo he still didn't see her until... When he walked up the steps and to the other side there she was lying down with a blanket over her. Standing over her he started to cry. Seeing her there he couldn't even bring himself to touch her, while she laid there so peaceful, he just sat down from exhaustion, and cried.

Then seemingly from heaven he heard a voice "are you okay dear?"

He reveled in the sound and with his eyes closed he said "Brenda, are you already speaking to me from the High Council?"

"No silly just from our gazebo."

He jumped up and yelled from the top of his lungs "YOU'RE, YOUR NOT DEAD!"

Knowing that he was in her dream last night she played with him a little and said "not yet, when do you want me to go?"

"Never!" he said.

"Well I think you understand that it won't be long."

"Why didn't they just take you last night? I thought they did! I was hoping and praying that they didn't."

"Funny how hope and prayer does work. Daanic was so touched with our show or Love for each other that they decided to wait one more season."

"So in the fall you will leave me?"

"Yes, and we will have this time to prepare everything for that transition."

They spent the rest of the day talking and enjoying the beautiful Earth they lived on. Brenda did write a song that morning, thinking about all that she had been told about her past life, and now where her future lies.

Another Time

Live many lives and in the process become
Something real that will never be undone
Sorting through it is purely meaningless

Then you find yourself in another time
Another time these changes even rhyme
Only then do you see that you will be

Hoping you find even more time here
Thinking that you know it all so clear
Believe it and you will come to know
The whole universe is only a big show

Become part of the plan so you can see
Life in different forms than you or me
Once put in the flow of eternity

Travelling through galaxies you embrace
Diverse possibilities of the human race
Coming together again you are one

Hoping you find even more time here
Thinking that you know it all so clear
Believe it and you will come to know
The whole universe is only a big show

Playing the role of what is given you
Not hard nor something to eschew
Adding life's emotions to the universe

Giving to time of yourself you see
Everything is given of pure energy
Light your way to write your verse

He read this and it made him feel better about what was
to happen in the fall. Not that he liked it but he looked forward to

learning about his past lives. In the next few months Brad will spend more time with Brenda in and out of their dreams. He will learn more about the High Council and be ready to help Rick on that day that Brenda leaves because Daisy will need both of their support.

CHAPTER 14

Sunny days and cool nights, this was a wonderful summer for Daisy and Rick. They are so in love and they can't seem to spend enough time together. Brenda and Brad learned so much about their lives on Millennia and the old Earth through their astral travel while dreaming. Knowing that they were both cardiologists and that they fell in love in a dream state was just so perfectly planned for them. Now Brenda is a politician just like her moms Tamla and Shasha and Brad is a farmer. They will use all of this knowledge they have gained to help Daisy and Rick during the summer.

"Okay Rick, you becoming a doctor is a great thing to be, but you will also need a hobby, what do you think you would want to do with your free time?"

Without batting an eye he said "spend it with Daisy."

Although Brad loved that answer he was a realist too and said "okay, after your first six months of marriage what then?"

He wasn't sure where this was going but he answered with "well I do like a fine wine and have been reading up on the business. Daisy and I like to go to the vineyards and look around while tasting their stock."

"Now we're getting somewhere, follow me." He walked him around the barn and they hopped into the electric golf cart and headed up the hill.

"Where are we going?"

Brad just smiled and shortly after that they went over the hill. There they were the vineyards and plenty of them. Rick knew right then and there what his hobby was going to be. He then said to Brad "this place is more than great, it's fantastic!"

"Yes it is, and I just love it up here, now let me show you around."

These two men were walking around the vines and inspecting the grapes and Brad made sure he described what type they were to Rick. He was especially proud of his noble red ones of merlot, cabernet sauvignon and Brenda's favorite the Pinot Noir. What made these wines so special were the grapes he would use. While some people would splice the grapes and create one of many to use, Brad never felt right about changing the grapes from their natural state.

Rick was caught up in all the knowledge that Brad had about growing grapes and making wine. He thought how this will be such a wonderful place to come to after he becomes a doctor. But for now he was more than willing to show up at least once a week to help Brad out and to learn all he can. He knew that there was no substitute for hands on experience.

Tasting several bottles of red, white and even eating some grapes they picked out a couple of bottles that had been aging for a few years and brought them back home. Brad told Rick to take a bottle of each back home with him.

"Ready?"

"Yep" Rick answered while holding up two bottles.

"Okay then let's go."

Driving down the hill Brad asked Rick about how he felt knowing that Daisy might be a politician one day. He didn't seem to mind and told Brad that his love for her was all that mattered. That was good enough for Brad and he thought with his new found knowledge of being a doctor in a previous life that maybe he could help Rick in school.

While Brad took Rick over the hill to show him his winery, Brenda was intent on teaching Daisy all about her becoming a good politician. Yes it is possible to be a good politician, she told Brad from time to time. He would always say that he knew she was a good one but... That's when she would cut him off and just say never mind. Now she has her granddaughter to teach before the summer ends.

"Daisy you will need to learn the magic from these books I will be using to teach you this summer."

"Grandma, why do say this summer, you talk like we don't have that much time to learn this?"

"Well dear I'm getting old and we just avoided a large war with the people of Sorentito. Not to mention our people from Tarmish can turn on us anytime now."

"Okay I see your point and I really like the songs you write. Do you think I'll ever get that type of talent?"

"Yes I do. All talent comes to us when we are in the flow of life, it's never late, and it's never early."

Brenda made sure that Daisy would go and get the law books (that are from Millennia) while in the study. The main thing Brenda was teaching her was how to take over and where to find the answers in the books of these laws.

Back in school this year will be the last year for Daisy and after she graduates with her law degree she plans on taking the bar exam. Then if successful she would like to be a state defender, well first she will work for the assistant. Not sure if she will run for political office anytime soon after that, although Brenda has been grooming her to run for office one day.

Today in class her classmates wanted to hear all about her time in Tarmish during the siege of the Sorentito's. Never to be rude she had the quality of being able to answer questions by giving out as little information as possible. Also doing that while making the person know how important they and their questions are to her. This showed her ability to handle a situation and leave the other person feeling better after conversing with her.

This last year is shaping up to be one of her best and after all that she's been through it's certainly welcomed. The time spent with her family of Vagan Masters at Plotinus' Pub is something she looks forward too again. Their table was going strong talking about the plans to give aide to the Sorentito people in order to prevent another war.

Gloria overheard them talking and she waited until she gathered enough information to then enter in. Walking up to the table she said "being kind and helping anyone in need is a high virtue. I would also like to submit that it is good to help, but if the recipient doesn't use the help to rectify the problem, and they only come back time after time again. Then this, "help" will become no help and can only make the problem worse."

The table sat dumbfounded with what she had said. So going to wait on another table, Gloria had her excuse to leave and let them discuss this. Daisy spoke up and said "okay I don't know if you know this but when a rescue team was sent to Tarmish for me and Julie this happened. After we were rescued and on our way back to Otium one of the three teams left a very large amount of supplies for the enemy and another team left them for Tarmish too."

A few of her friends started talking between each other and then one said "why did we leave supplies for the enemy? I mean what good could that possibly accomplish?"

"Good question" Daisy said. Then she wanted to know if there were any ideas as to why.

Still some more deliberation and another friend said "was it a show of friendship on our part?"

"Yes, it certainly was and that was definitely a part of the plan, and it caused them to do something important."

The same girl felt inspired to answer again, and she did so rather enthusiastically when she said "they took the supplies and went home to share with their people!"

"Right you are and..."

Another friend said "which freed Tarmish from the siege!"

"Exactly, now you're getting it. We need to do what's right always and then use that to our advantage."

Hearing the ruckus at Daisy's table gave Gloria another reason to return and say "what's going on over here?"

Daisy answered "just solving problems past and present."

"Oh really, what about the one I left you to solve?"

"You mean the one about help becoming no help at all?"

"Correct now what's the answer?"

The girl who had answered Daisy's question said what Daisy said before "we always do what's right and we use that to our advantage."

Gloria was so pleased watching Daisy take charge of the table, it was very inspiring, and she will let Brenda know about that, too.

When she's with Rick all these things change, she stops being a future politician, and becomes a future doctor's wife. Being the spouse of a successful doctor is something many people would feel honored to be. She loved him so much and did feel the honor of being his wife one day. So tonight she would just practice and look and play the part.

"Oh Rick how was school today" she said with a yawn.

Chuckling he said "well it wasn't as boring as your yawn implies it was."

"I'm sorry we had some intense deliberations at Plotinus' after class today."

"No problem, school was fine we are starting to learn a few surgery procedures."

"Well I can drink to you learning them and you will be an excellent surgeon if you ever decide to be."

"Thank you dear, I really enjoyed our week end on the farm. I've been thinking a lot about your grandpa's winery. It is something I want to do with some of my spare time."

"I liked working with him over the years so maybe we can do that together?"

He lifted his glass of a seven year vintage cabernet and said "a toast, to us working together in our own winery one day."

"I'll drink to that."

It's a strange way of living when you aren't sick with something incurable but you know that your time is limited. What do I mean by this statement is; Brenda knew that she would leave her body sometime in the fall. Before that her time with Brad, Daisy and the Assembly were so intense that she made sure to get the most out of every second. She drove some crazy with her ambition, but only Brad knew why, and he wouldn't say.

The leaves have turned to their magnificent colours and the air is cool and sweet. School is in full swing and Daisy is in her last year. Brenda is so pleased with her progress and she feels that she will be a great politician one day.

Brad has used every day to consciously cherish Brenda as much as he can and to love her deeper than ever before. Sometimes she would joke about running away if he didn't tone it down, but she understood. He knew that this wasn't exactly a joke and did his best to back off a little. The thought of life without her was not an option in his mind and his heart was in total agreement to love her all it could.

Schedules are meant to be kept, but there are times that they should be altered, and with the world relatively at peace this allowed her to tone back her time in the Assembly. One thing she did do in secret was to pick and to then groom her successor. Knowing that it would be Herthro she made sure he was ready and he didn't know why but he did enjoy the extra attention he was receiving from her.

Evenings at the farm were filled with great cooking, some discussion and plenty of love. On the week-ends Brenda required that Daisy and Rick stay at least one night and Rick couldn't get enough time in the winery with Brad. Daisy knew that her political life was being formed in the best way by the greatest leader she had ever known. They would also spend some time with the boys in the winery during those weekends.

All the while Brenda would have dreams and Brad would be there too. It would take place on Millennia or on some occasions it would be at the High Council. During these dreams they would learn so much about their past and how what the rest on Earth believed about their three planets was just to give them a new start. This did take some time to fully comprehend but once they understood that life is a continuum of the universe they proceeded on well in their ascension.

In their last dream things seemed to be winding down and Brad was talking with Tamla about how he wasn't sure if his heart would be able to make it without Brenda. That's when Tamla really showed her knowledge and Love that she has gained over the years by putting her arm around him. She said "son when she comes up here to be with us she will have ascended to another level in her Spirit..."

"But... I don't want to be without her. Why can't we both go together? Is that too much to ask?"

"No. Brad it's never wrong to ask for something from your heart. You need to know this; that we are never given more than we can handle in any of our existences."

He looked over at Brenda while Daanic was teaching her and seeing the excitement on her face gave him the answer. Not the complete answer but one enough to push him in that direction. Then he turned back to Tamla and said "what could I receive that would help me through this?"

"You will visit her once a week or if you ask for another time. Her Spirit will reside in yours to make your heart warm and calm."

"Well if you say so I will have to be strong and use whatever tools are given to me."

When he woke after this dream he found her still in bed and this made the sunrise the most impressive site to see and share with the one he loved the most. That day was spent without her for the better part because she had business in the Assembly and while she was gone he would think about all that Tamla told him. Then he would practice the feelings of having her Spirit in his heart and this gave him a lot of hope.

Control is that what this is? Well since Brenda called on them Tamla and Shasha have been consciously involved in her life. Now that they are ready to have her return to their home, a plan will need to be made. Because Shasha said to Tamla "we can't have him wake up and then see that she has left her body. I remember what that was like too many times and I won't be a part of it with our daughter."

"Okay what do you suppose we should do?'

"I think we should include her in this. We can give her an opportunity to say her goodbyes."

This evening she would visit them in her dream, but Brad won't be there.

"Mom what is going on?" Brenda said to Shasha.

"Well dear we need to plan your final day on Earth."

"Is that why Brad is not here?"

'Yes I want to talk with you about how you can leave your body without having him wake up and see that you are gone."

Brenda was definitely taken this all in and said "now that's an interesting challenge. I never dreamed that I would be able to plan my own death."

Tamla said "dear, I have been coming up with a plan while you were talking with Shasha."

"Okay mom, then give it to us..."

She then woke up without the answer just knowing that her moms are planning it and that Brad will not be there.

So much information and so little time and although she didn't know the day or the hour she did know that it was near. Watching Daisy and Rick made her think about her and Brad's love that started so many hundreds of years ago. Tonight during dinner with Brad was so special and for some reason she felt being that young again. By the end of dinner Brad had some news to tell her.

During the pouring of some more wine, passing her the plate of cheese, and chips, Brad said "Rick called me today" then waited for her question.

"Oh what did he have to say?"

"He called to invite us to dinner on Friday?"

Brenda had chill bumps go down her arms and Brad could see them. She said "he's popping the question!"

Brad smiled and said "I like to say it this way; he's going to ask her to marry him."

Laughing she said "same thing." Then she put her glass down on the table so fast she almost knocked it over and not remembering the day she said "when?"

Just enjoying her excitement he said "this Friday."

A few days have passed and it's Wednesday night their plans for dinner are routine. He called her an hour before the date and asked if they could change the location. Not knowing what he was up to she agreed and asked where? Telling her that a fellow student told him about an Italian restaurant on the beach and that this was a place he wanted to try.

Tonight he would pick her up and when she looked out the window there was a limousine! Walking up the stairs he went and knocked on the door. The door opens and she says "a limousine what are you up to Mr. Brackett?"

"Just giving my girl the elegance she deserves."

Going with the flow was all she could do and this was a very cool river to ride down tonight. He opened her door and helped with her long beautiful teal green dress. A dress he requested that she wear.

A crescent moon in the sky reflected on the sea where the waves were calm. With the evening just starting and they had about thirty minutes before their reservations. Rick opened her door and asked "would you like to walk on the boardwalk with me?"

"Of course I would" she then took his hand and off they went.

He had thought about this for a few weeks now. Drinking the wine on the week ends with Brad brought on some good conversations and one of them was tonight. Rick had a lot of respect for Brad and valued his opinion very much because Brad was a gentleman. Brad's advice will be carried out tonight.

Holding her hand and thinking about how lucky he was especially if hopefully the answer is yes. He walked her to the end of the pier where the sailboats were tied up. Then like a ballroom dancer he spun her around and held on to both of her hands. She looked stunned at his aggression and then felt so much of the love in the air tonight.

Down on one knee he went, and to her surprise, this took her breath away. He then reached into his inside coat pocket and pulled out a small green box. As he opened the box she thought her heart was going to stop and then the excitement climaxed when he said "Daisy Cole will you marry me?"

This one answer she had rehearsed over and over and now was her chance to say it "yes Mr. Richard Brackett I would be honored to marry you."

Before he could stand up she grabbed him and gave him a kiss that he will remember all this evening. They walked into the restaurant to have dinner and only one glass of wine each because this evening will be filled with dining, dancing, and a future together that can only be imagined. Throughout this night she just couldn't take her eyes off of this marvelous ring.

It didn't take long for Brenda to get the news, because Daisy sent her a text when Rick went to the washroom. This just made the summer seem so much more special to have spent with Rick and to get to know who he is. Looking at Brad lying in bed she said "you knew all along that he was going to ask the question didn't you?"

Rolling over with a sheepish grin he said "no, I knew that he was going to ask her to marry him."

"Ha, that's the same thing. What did he say to you?"

"Well we talked about this for a few weeks now and he wanted to know when would be the best time to ask her. At first he wanted to do it at the end of the evening and I told him no you need to ask her in the most romantic setting possible. Then he told me where he was taking her for dinner and dancing. I told him to walk her along the pier and that's where he should ask her, this will make the rest of the evening magical."

"Well I'm so happy it's like something on my bucket list being checked. Hey I guess I should start a list."

"We will see them on Friday and you can tell them how happy you are."

Friday couldn't get there fast enough for Brenda or for Daisy. Rick took Brads advice about arranging the dinner two nights after asking Daisy to marry him. This gave the girls a couple of days to cool down.

There is a cafe' downtown in one of the skyscrapers and he mentioned it to Brad. Brad had told Rick then, that he had wanted to go up there for dinner but could never find the time. This was an invitation so he couldn't pass up the opportunity he thought to himself. Parking outside of the city on the loop there were many places to park and ride the rails in. This was something Brad wanted to do because being on the farm he didn't have a reason to do that.

Looking out the big glass window Brad said "what a wonderful view of the sea and from 54 floors up you could see a lot of the sea" he really liked the way that sounded.

"Funny grandpa, now that was a funny rhyme."

"I try."

The evening was joyous and the girls talked about how their men proposed to them and what they said. The men talked a lot about growing grapes and making wine and of course they talked about when the marriage will be and Daisy had always talked about having it in the spring.

A wedding in the spring when you knew that you won't be on this earth past the fall is what Brenda had to deal with. Although Brad wished it wasn't so he couldn't say anything to Daisy for this was her special day. To then be alone on that day without Brenda he did feel sad but honored to be there to walk his granddaughter down the aisle.

Both of them made sure that they wouldn't let the wonder of this evening become tarnished with anything negative. They talked and talked about the wedding plans and even Brad and Rick picked out the wines they would serve. Daisy told her grandma "I want lots of flowers."

Returning to the farm after such a wonderful time Brenda was happy but, sad too. He didn't know what to do, but try as he might her emotions would go up and down. First it was how happy she was that Daisy was marrying such a great man and knowing that her granddaughter's wedding will be so beautiful in the spring. Once all this sat in, she came to the reality that she will not be there for it, and then down came the tears.

The night was troubling for her, as she tossed and turned, and then during the night she would ask her moms if she could join them. Shasha was the first to say yes without asking Tamla, Tamla just smiled because she learned a long time ago, that when Shasha wanted to protect their little girl, you don't try to stop her. Talking with them calmed her down so Brad could get some rest he did have a big day planned on the farm and he needed to start bringing in the harvest.

Who You Don't See

Wedding bells make a sound so sweet
And it isn't that they are only for one
Being with her and all would be neat

Giving to this one love you bring
Lovely so lovely you are so sweet
All together on this day of spring

What you don't see

Are always for you
The eyes of me

This our gift we give that we love
Wonder of all is to become today
Live a life from below and above

Your endeavors will not be a bust
Live a life as all in love will do
Find peace, joy, hope and to trust

What you don't see
Are always for you
The eyes of me

Blessed you've learned how to serve
Watching from near or from far I do
I'm seeing this life that you deserve

Out of my Spirit for you I give
I will do from another dimension
Not from the planet that you live

What you don't see
Are always for you
The eyes of me

My Spirit will reside in you
You can feel that I'm there
This magic is all that we do

To not know where I have been
I serve, love and give to them all

For you will visit me once again

What you don't see
Are always for you
The eyes of me

CHAPTER 15

Intelligence came in that there was a military build-up north of Tarmish. This was not good news and it needed to be disseminated out to the Assembly. Herthro read through it and asked all the appropriate questions of their scouts that were there. As he looked at the pictures, videos, and military assessments it became clear that Sorentito was preparing for another attack. He quickly realized that it was now time to bring in the High Councilor to devise a plan of action.

The text came in on her secured, encrypted line, and she was asked to tune her video device to a special frequency that also was protected. While doing this she was currently in her study alone and ready to hear from the Assembly's Military council. As she spotted Herthro on the screen she said "Herthro what is the emergency you contacted for?"

"Your Grace we have confirmed reports that King Barborda's people are amassing a large military force less than 600 kilometers north of Tarmish."

"Okay so I'm to assume that the full Military Affairs Council is now assembled?"

"Yes Your Grace we are now awaiting your arrival to direct us and to formulate a plan."

"Alright then send me your summary and I'll be there first thing tomorrow afternoon."

"Yes I will, Your Grace."

"That will be all Herthro."

Staying in her office for a few hours more she needed to familiarize herself with the information. Knowing that she was called for something urgent Brad knew that she will come out when she's done. He was a very patient man so when she stepped out he didn't bother her, but rather she came to him, and she said "I have to travel to the Assembly tomorrow for some urgent business."

"Okay and I won't ask what for. I probably don't want to know anyway."

There will be no dream travel tonight just sleep, deep sleep. Brad did dream about some grapes he has been trying to cultivate to grow for a special blend he's concocting. The sun came up he had breakfast ready for her and a kiss goodbye and off she went.

Herthro was waiting outside for her arrival, so when her car pulled up he then quickly opened her door, and rushed her inside. Once inside he said "Your Grace we are being very careful because we believe there might be spies in the area."

"How do you know that?"

"We discussed some low level information that was in the intelligence community. We used that to set up a sting, to find out where it came from, and the only leads we have are in this area."

"Good work we will then need to do a security sweep of my office before we meet there."

"Already done Your Grace" he said.

"Good then do another one."

In the meeting she looked at all the videos and photos from the area of the build-up. In the room many ideas flowed, some were from plans they did before and others were combinations of the new ideas. One plan was to negotiate with them again by leaving a large supply of needed goods. Although this was still a very viable option, Brenda said "I like all of your ideas, but I'm not sure what we should do yet."

Herthro said "Your Grace we know you'll come up with something you always do."

'Thank you Herthro, I did come up with some ideas last night so here they are, maybe some of you can improve on them, and we can all find one that will work."

"I'm certain we will Your Grace, thank you."

Sharing her ideas did spark many thoughts and improvements and they did come up with a plan. Now for the best part of the plan... the diversion!

This diversion is to send the High Councilor to Tarmish and await a meeting with King Barborda that was currently being arranged. She packed up some things and then loaded them into her car along with her entourage. Studying this plan over and over and not feeling right about how much of a deception it was. This had kept her up late thinking, which made her very tired, and so she took a nap on the drive there.

Arriving at the headquarters with her consort Herthro they went upstairs and settled into their office. Waiting for the information to come back regarding a possible meeting with King Barborda they were not surprised that there was no word back today. She looked over at Herthro, smiled, shrugged her shoulders and said "let's go get some dinner, I'm starved."

"Sounds good Your Grace let's go."

They finished dinner and then had some discussion on the possible preceding meeting. Brenda was still very tired and didn't know what she would say to King Barborda and the plan they came up with was sketchy at best but she did grudgingly approve it.

Tonight she tried to stay awake late but the stress of the day tapped her energy and before getting ready for bed she did have some facetime with Brad. Needing nothing to help her sleep, when her head hit the pillow, she was out like a light. Travelling in a dream she seemed wide awake and feeling energized, now that she was back in the High Council. Looking around and finding Tamla and Shasha there with her she asked them "where is Brad?"

"He's not here dear" Tamla said to her.

"What do you mean he's not here?"

Feeling responsible for this Shasha spoke up and said "this was my idea. I did this because when he was here before with you, and you two found out together that you will be coming back soon for good, he didn't take it too well."

"So you wanted to spare him, his feelings?" she said not angry but just in a curious manner.

Tamla said "yes, and tonight you aren't going back to your body."

"Well mom, I did figure that out" she said with a laugh.

There was a big announcement from Leto that Brenda was now welcomed back to the High Council as an elder just like her great grandmother Jillela (Terames aka Elizabeth) was before.

In the morning Herthro knocked and knocked on her door but no answer. He first thought that maybe she was in the restroom and gave her an hour to finish. Then from his room he called her and no answer even on her smart phone!

Waiting another hour and still no contact he then proceeded downstairs to the lobby. There he convinced the manager to bring the master key and travel upstairs to her room. As they opened the door and called her name there was no answer. Then they noticed her lying in her bed all curled up. Herthro spoke very softly and said "Brenda do you want to sleep a little longer?"

Still with no answer the manager walked over to him, handed him a mirror and he knew what to do with it. After placing it in front of her nose and noticing no steam, sadly he had his answer. The first thing that went through his mind was how to tell Brad. That would be something that he and the team will need to talk about on their way home.

One thing that was a pleasant surprise was that King Barborda's people returned the message for their meeting. His message was that it wasn't needed and that the supplies that they were given will do for now. King Barborda took his army and returned home. Herthro did the same thing, now with his new entourage.

The acting High Councilor Herthro will get the credit for solving the latest emergency. Brenda is very happy that he will be confirmed as the next leader of the Tres Vagan people and the first thing on his new agenda will be to talk with Brad privately. This is not something that he relishes doing. He quickly sent Brad a message that he wants to meet with him in two days and when Brad asked about Brenda, Herthro replied that he wasn't at liberty to say anything right now.

A day later and Herthro arrives by himself to their farm and walking into the house he looks grimly at Brad. There are some welcome exchanges and then Herthro said to him "can we meet in her study? This needs to be done in private."

"Sure we can do that, follow me."

As they both sat down poor Herthro looked so nervous. Then while taking a deep breath in, an idea came to him, so he said "can we spend some time in quiet meditation?"

"Okay let's do that" Brad said to him in a put off tone and also a worried one.

"Thanks."

The room was quiet their eyes were closed and they both took in deep breaths. Herthro knew that he needed to clear his mind and to receive some universal courage. While the time went on Brad went deep into himself and communicated with Brenda's Spirit in his heart. Time went longer than normal and then Brad opened his eyes and said "my friend I know that she's gone."

Stunned Herthro said "how did you know?"

"She just told me a few minutes ago and I'm fine with it."

Talk about the weight of the world taken from upon your shoulders. He never felt so blessed to not have to give such horrible news to Brad. Looking up at the sun with his arm around Brad he said "thank you Brenda your power transcends all dimensions."

Herthro left and Brad went back to working on the farm and all during the day he would feel her everywhere he went. Taking care of all the plowing that he needed to do, he would later travel to his winery, and spend hours there with his grapes. All day he would talk with her as if she was there with him.

Rick and Daisy will be there the next day and he knew he would need to tell her then about her being gone. This wouldn't be easy but he thought that this might just send Daisy further on her path in Grandma's footsteps. He went home and spent a few hours in meditation because he felt so much closer to her then.

On the heels of the wedding announcement and all the plans that she made with her grandma Daisy was eager to see her. Driving there she talked Rick's ear off but he didn't mind he loved it when she was excited about anything good. Unloading the car Rick noticed Brad walk out and then Daisy took off and went inside. Brad walked over to Rick and said "she's gone Rick."

"What do you mean she's gone?"

"Just that, Brenda has left her body and is no longer a part of our dimension."

Rick liked him putting it that way since he was heavily into quantum physics and he said "okay we need to tell Daisy right?"

"Unfortunately we do."

This weekend they spent a lot of time talking about how much Brenda meant to them and that they wished she didn't have to leave. Brad did a lot of consoling by explaining to them that she is an elder in the High Council of the Pleiades. This didn't really mean that much to them but knowing that she was on her universal path did.

Daisy spent the week end with Brad and Rick in the winery. This will now become a larger part of the time spent visiting Brad. Although the boys did enjoy her company, and she learned quite a lot about the grapes, this wasn't what she wanted to be spending most of her time doing. Then one day she was contacted by Herthro who is now the newly elected High Councilor. As they talked he invited her to visit him at the Assembly. Enjoying the teaching's that he would give her she then asked if he would visit her on Brad's farm.

This time the boys were surprised because she did not want to spend time with them in the winery. Instead shortly after arriving there Herthro showed up to spend a day and night. She immediately took him to her grandma's study and showed him all the books from their home (Millennia). Brenda taught her where to find the books that contained the answers to any problems that might arise. Doing this was something that Brenda had made her promise to do.

Daisy was still in her last year of college and the pub was a regular stop after school. There she and her friends would discuss all of the political actions that had taken place and ones that might need to in the future. Gloria would look after her like she was her granddaughter now and while in deep meditation Gloria would sometimes channel Brenda. During her conversations with Brenda, Gloria would be given instructions on what Daisy needed to learn.

At the farm this time Daisy invited Gloria to visit with her. Weeks spent with Herthro were very useful for Daisy. There she learned from him, and now he has access to Brenda's study. Daisy wanted to bring another Master to the farm, and Gloria was a welcomed addition. Because Daisy needed her to help her understand the things that Brenda had taught her before.

As months went by these people would spend more and more time together learning and becoming closer as only a family could. Brad would look forward to his dreams with Brenda once a week and amazingly he handled her departing a lot better than he thought he would.

As she watched them come together and help one another she was so inspired. Brad would teach Rick all he could about farming. They spent many hours growing the grapes, putting them into barrels, and then bottling them into wine. Daisy would split her time with Herthro and Gloria. One would help with government, the other in mastery of the mind, and with the environment around her.

The one thing that really piqued her interest was how the presence of Gloria on the farm seemed to stir gentlemanly feelings in Brad. Brenda was becoming very knowledgeable of her duties as an elder and taking her tablet she decided to write a song about this new family that was being formed.

Not just blood

Being with you this we choose
No matter where you were born
We will love you win or loose
From us you will not be torn

Loved like I love the universe
To give back all they could
Your love was never my curse
Called to leave that I would

We are blood, we are water
We are Spirit, in this order
We can love, we can hate
We have to believe to relate

When one leaves it's not forever
Meditate, feel them inside to start
This time we will all be together
Know they reside inside your heart

Give love out to build this bridge
So all will walk across and to feel

A heart beating out on this ridge
Love again and to know it's real

We are blood, we are water
We are Spirit, in this order
We can love, we can hate
We have to believe to relate

Open these doors and welcome all
You will see them then come anew
This family will love and not fall
Love only comes from what you do

We are blood, we are water
We are Spirit, in this order
We can love, we can hate
We have to believe to relate

CHAPTER 16

Vagan Masters are becoming less and less needed, only in Otium do a few live now, and their teaching has ended. Daisy has decided to continue her education and pursue a law degree. Rick works on his school and supports Daisy anyway he can. He has also made secret plans for after their wedding. These plans involve where they will reside and she has all but talked him into building a little cottage on the farm. To her way of thinking this is so they can be there to help her grandpa.

On this day there seemed to be something special in the air for Brad, Daisy, Rick, Herthro, and Gloria. They have been spending a lot of time together on the farm lately. There are a lot of little indications that this group of people are really bonding together as a family. Now this doesn't mean that they don't have their own families outside of this group, because some do, but what is happening here is very exciting.

"Grandpa, how are you doing? I'm so sorry we couldn't make it last weekend, we needed to study for our finals?" This Daisy said while giving him a big hug.

He then extended his arms up and said "That's okay sweetie Gloria stopped by to visit and we had a wonderful time."

With a smile Rick looked at her and then grabbed the bags from the trunk, she took hold his hand and her bag from him as they walked into the house. This visit will be very busy because their wedding is less than ten days away and she has the time down to the minute. For help getting all the plans together and for making sure they all will work Gloria has volunteered her time.

A funny thing happened when these three sat down to talk about the wedding. Brad was full of questions to ask them and one of those he asked was "Daisy you've decided to pursue a law degree? Do you plan on passing the bar and becoming a lawyer?"

"I'm not sure grandpa, but I think Gloria mentioned that it would help me in politics."

This conversation really got them thinking and Rick said "I think she's going to follow in her grandma's footsteps."

A few more questions on this and they would only help to confirm her main goal of being just like her grandma. Brad would tell her that even as wonderful as Brenda was, he felt that she will exceed many of those accomplishments that Brenda achieved.

Daisy said "thanks grandpa, you are so kind. It's so good to see that you are doing well, but remember, we will be are here to help you whenever you call."

Rick said "Brad you do seem to be in good spirits is there something you want to share with us?"

'Nothing I can think of Rick just trying to make the best of my life."

This made Daisy feel really good because she was worried about her grandpa. Knowing how much Brenda meant to him and to lose her with no indication of something being wrong was a lot to handle. So with that information she didn't understand how he could be so cheerful but she wasn't complaining. If anything she knew that her grandma would be so happy to see him this way.

Their conversation went away from talking about Brenda and shifted to the upcoming wedding. Brad went into the kitchen to get a bottle of wine and a plate of crackers and cheese that he had made earlier. Rick then said to Daisy "when is Gloria supposed to arrive here?"

"I'm not sure maybe I should contact her."

Before she could send a text to Gloria, Brad walked back in and started pouring some wine for all. Looking over at her and seeing her texting on her tablet he said "who are you texting?"

"I'm texting Gloria asking when she thinks she'll get here."

A big smile was on his face, not one of a joke, but a smile like he was in love. They really didn't know what to think until he then asked rather eagerly "what did she say?"

"I don't know grandpa she hasn't..."

Her words were interrupted when Brad's phone rang and he answered it and said "hello."

He didn't say anything else but "goodbye see ya soon."

Then almost in unison, Rick and Daisy said "who was that?"

He chuckled and took a deep breath and said "just Gloria."

Daisy said "well, when did she say she will be here?"

"She said soon, less than an hour."

The table went silent, and this wasn't an uncomfortable feeling, but instead a very peaceful one. They had some small talk about the wedding location and how the dress alterations came out. Then after some laughter Daisy said "no Rick you can't see the dress until grandpa walks me down the aisle."

"I know and I wouldn't dream of asking you to do that."

Times flies when you're laughing and joking around until the front door opens. There she was all ready to spend the weekend with the bride to be, but before Rick could even think to get up and help her inside, Brad was already doing just that. So Daisy put her hand on top of Rick's and she said "boy he's fast."

"I know" Rick said and then putting his hand on his chin finished that thought with "maybe there's more to this."

After sitting her down at the table Brad cleared his throat and said "what are you two talking about and what's with the grin?"

"Nothing grandpa, it's nothing" she said with a smile then before anyone could talk, she said very blushingly "Gloria I'm so glad you made it today."

"I wouldn't miss this special day to help you with your wedding for the world." She thought about mentioning how sad it was that Brenda wasn't there but, both she and Daisy understood that.

The girls started talking about all the dresses, flowers, music and etcetera that were going to be in the wedding. Brad and Rick stayed for as long as they could until Rick said "let's go look at those grapes we planted last week."

"Good idea! I believe hanging around these two will destroy our manhood if we aren't too careful."

Gloria gave Brad that look of a school girl blushing about something funny that her soon to be boyfriend might have said. Putting down the box of bows that she was looking through, Daisy's eyes became a bit wider, but she said nothing. It was in that moment she suspected something was going on between these two, and she liked that idea very much.

Once they were long gone out the door Daisy looked at Gloria and said "you like him don't you?'

"Huh!" she was dumbfounded but then realized how she had acted had said it all. That's when she felt that Daisy needed to know her feelings for her grandpa and said "yes I do, I'm sorry I know, I ..."

"Stop right there Missy, I can't think of a more caring, loving person for my grandpa to fall in love with, but you."

"What are you saying do you think he likes me too?"

"Of course he does Gloria and why wouldn't he?"

What to do with this information was all that filled Gloria's mind. Knowing how she felt about him didn't change the fact that she was there to help Daisy. Now it was time to put all those feelings aside and do just that. Walking over to Daisy and giving her a hug, she said "let's get your wedding taken care of, shall we?"

"Sounds like a plan I'm sure grandpa will find a way to let you know how he feels."

Planning this day to a "T" was their goal and Brenda left her a very large dowry to do it with. These people aren't extravagant with resources, no quite the contrary and this will probably be her only wedding in this lifetime. The feeling is to make it as memorable as can be for all involved.

Things were really falling into place and Daisy did not realize what an organizer Gloria was. Realizing that Gloria owns the pub that she loves to hang out in with her college friends, makes perfect sense to her, and that she couldn't be any happier now to have her help.

It was time to start thinking about dinner and that's when Daisy came up with an incredible idea. Remembering the place that Rick took her to propose, she thought what a great place for some dinner, and dancing. Maybe with the atmosphere and the environment being so right her grandpa might make his feelings known to Gloria there?

They put away all their things neatly into the boxes that were clearly labeled. Then closing a box, that they had put together on the computer, she stopped and said "Gloria let's go out for some dinner and dancing tonight. I feel very happy and excited that we accomplished what we needed to do today."

"Where do you want to go?"

"The same restaurant that Rick proposed to me at is where I want to go tonight. I love that place and I want to share it with you and grandpa."

Concerned that she didn't have anything dressy to wear tonight had caused Gloria to believe that she couldn't go. That's when Daisy took her by the hand and led her into her room to the closet. They weren't too different in size so she said to her "pick out an outfit and get ready cause' we're going."

Gloria grabbed her so tight and hugged her and said "I love you Daisy girl."

Barely able to breathe Daisy said "I love you too Gloria, just let me breathe please."

Gloria released her and they both laughed until they cried happy tears. Daisy sent a text to Rick explaining to him that she and Gloria decided that they were going to dinner tonight and also dancing. Reading that he chuckled and in his text he said "I see that you two have been plotting up there while we were bottling wine."

"Look at what Rick wrote" she said to Gloria holding her tablet.

Putting her hand on Daisy's shoulder she said "well we sure have, haven't we."

The boys rode up to the house to get ready for tonight's activities. On the ride up Brad asked Rick about this place that they were going too, and told him that he had never been there before. All the information he needed was given by Rick and this seemed to settle Brad's nerves a little. Happy and content Brad said "you are a big help around here. I do hope this place gives you a lot of peace from your duties as a doctor."

"I'm sure it will and I really like that plot we looked at today for the cottage we will build. The views are spectacular and I can't wait to show Daisy tomorrow."

Laughing and tapping the wheel Brad said "yes the views of the vineyards are great there too!"

With a sheepish grin he said "what else is there to look at?"

"Better not start off with that when you show it to her tomorrow. I would emphasize the hills and the lake first."

"Good idea."

This day could be titled "The Longest Day" except that was an old World War II movie from the previous Earth age. So no titles just getting on with the events that are so marvelously scripted, did I say scripted well maybe they are just a little by Daisy. Gloria knows that she is doing this and she is in complete agreement.

Quickly everyone is dressed for the evening and they were ready to drive off to the restaurant. Rick and Daisy are in the front seats with Gloria and Brad sitting in the back. Brad opens the door for her and then guides her into the car. Once inside he smiles at her and then she returns the gesture by softly looking into his eyes. In this magical evening they are starting it off like a couple of teenagers going on a first date and he thought boy does she smell good.

Getting out of the car Rick took Daisy by the hand and walked her back to the boardwalk where he first proposed to her. Then he turned and motioned for Brad to bring Gloria along with him to follow them. Turning to smile at Daisy, she just nodded at him then turned around and headed to the end of the pier. After arriving there Rick turned around looked at them and said "this is where she said yes."

Call it courage or call it the eagerness of the moment, but that's when Brad reached down, and held Gloria's hand. Sparks then flew in her heart and she thought its beating so loudly they must hear it because it's drowning out my hearing.

As an experienced woman, she knew not to make a move but to let things progress further and the evening was still so young that they haven't even had dinner yet.

Dinner was perfect some seafood and a very fine bottle of chardonnay. Even with such great company there wasn't a lot of talking just enjoying the food and the wine. This evening was later filled with talking and discussion about many things about how they were going to enjoy life together. Their conversations did vary but after the wine was finished they just let the Spirit move them.

The music did have something to do with their mood tonight, especially when the band played something slow, immediately Rick took Daisy's hand, and escorted her to the dance floor. He looked over at Brad, nodded his head to encourage him, and Brad got the message. He stood up, walked over to her, reached for her hand, and said "Gloria may I have this dance?"

Progress is moving right along and she will not get in the way. In fact she was more than willing to ride down this river of love tonight. With a beautiful smile she said "I would be honored to dance with such a gentleman."

Taking her hand and placing his right one behind her shoulder, yes he knew how to dance. The difference was that this beautiful woman was not his wife of several hundred years and it was a change for him. But shortly after he started the steps, she just fell right into place, and his heart couldn't tell the difference. A still soft voice in his heart made a sound like Brenda and said "everything is fine you need and deserve someone."

Still taking it slowly, he decided to sit down for a couple of songs with Gloria sitting there next to him, and with a small but visible smile Gloria was very happy. The others joined them for a rest but after a few songs they all decided to go back and dance some more. This one was a tango and they were having so much fun giggling and moving about that at the end of this one Brad asked her "would you like to take a walk?"

"I would love to."

Giving her his arm to take, he then escorted her out the door to the boardwalk, there she leaned forward and kissed him on the check. They were now walking under the stars and noticing how they all seemed to dance in the night sky. She released her hand from his arm and then placed it around his waist. She said "yes" very softly, held him a little closer, and leaned her head on his shoulder. Reaching the end of the pier they stopped, looking out over the water, he looked at her, and said "beautiful, simply beautiful."

"Yes this whole night is beautiful."

Then he turned to her and looked into her brown eyes and although it was dark he still remembered what they looked like. With a smile he said "I meant how beautiful you are." Then she kissed him!

The evening didn't end there it went on until the next morning and soon the farm will have another couple that are in love live there again, very soon. Rick showed Daisy the plot of land where they will build their cottage and she loved it. He took Brad's advice and didn't mention the vineyards, but when he was done talking she did say "and the vineyards are so pretty out there too" then she winked at him.

Daisy is back in school, and she knows that her wedding is only a day away, but this fact does not make Daisy nervous. Because she and Gloria had everything planned out. Skipping the pub tonight, she went straight to the farm after school to spend time preparing. First thing in the morning she will start to prepare herself for the wedding. Gloria will work with all the contractors, by showing them where to bring their goods, and to start setting them up. Rick showed up that evening and he too had his list of things to take care of for Daisy.

As Brad would travel in his dreams once a week he would learn and remember many things from his previous lives before. One of these things was who the High Councilor of the Pleiades Daanic was on the old Earth, and that her name was Margo, who is also Brenda's grandmother.

Brenda has a new name which is her old name from before on the High Council, she is now called Seliah. This is her old name from before her first time on Earth. Now she has been reunited with everyone there, both family and friends. A glorious reconnection with her grandpa Paul and many memories of being a doctor just like him on Earth. The one memory she cherished the most was her time at the Wizard's castle with Paul and especially that day she met Brad (Bradly then).

Tonight was the night before the big wedding. Seliah thought it would be the right time to welcome them to her universe. Brad invited Gloria to stay with him and she was happy to oblige. They're all at the farm and before they went to bed Brad asked if they could all spend some time drinking tea and meditating before turning in for the night.

The trees weren't completely green or full of leaves yet. Daisy picked the spring because she liked the cool temperature and the leaves still had many different colours. Tonight the wind would blow from the north and with the windows cracked open a little that cool wind would sweep in. Seliah had requested in a dream that Brad have them all there this night, she also asked him to make the tea, and lead in the meditation.

"Brenda, my darling how are you doing tonight?"

"Couldn't be better Brad, my new name is Seliah. This was my name long before I ever was born on Earth."

"Well okay I'll have to get use to that one. What are we doing tonight? I am a little surprised to be here before tomorrow."

"My dear Brad our granddaughter is getting married tomorrow and I want to give her my blessing."

"How are you going to..." then before he could finish that thought there she was.

"Hello grandpa what is going on? Is this for real or a dream?"

"It's a dream that's real, we have astral traveled."

"Traveled to where?"

"The Pleiades, we are at the High Council. This is where your grandma went after leaving her body."

Daisy was spellbound she just couldn't seem to comprehend it all. Shortly after looking around she heard a familiar voice. "Daisy what is going on?"

"I don't know" she told Rick as he stood there with his mouth wide open.

Seliah walked over to them, then Daisy ran to her and cried "grandma!" Grabbing her with a big hug, she asked "is this really you?"

"It's really me but just in another dimension."

"Another dimension, what's that mean?"

"It's a bit confusing, but I'm sure Rick can explain it to you later."

This evening was spent getting to know what Seliah has been up to since leaving Earth. There with Gloria in the dream and seeing how happy Brad was made this so much easier for her. Seliah told Gloria that she thought it was a perfect thing for them to become one, and that the day will come when all people will be that again. Brad was happy that she accepted Gloria as his new friend and probably his next wife.

When Gloria heard that, she said "is this for real or just a dream?"

Brad told her "this is for real, I can ask you tonight or we can wait until after Daisy and Rick's wedding tomorrow?"

"Let's wait we have too much to contend with as it is."

That settled that, they went on to meet Daanic the High Councilor, and her story was told to them by Brad as he remembered it. Tamla and Shasha were there and both gave Daanic their updates from Millennia. They also met Daisy who is their great-granddaughter and she loved them both.

Daisy didn't want this night to end, except to marry her wonderful fiancé, Rick, and to then spend the rest of their lives together. The sun was up and so was Brad, he went downstairs to make the coffee. This morning he figured that they would all need strong coffee to digest all that happened last night. While in the kitchen and looking in the refrigerator he heard this sweet voice say "did you mean what you said in your dream last night?"

Knowing who's beautiful voice that was, he said "every damn word of it."

Turning the corner to see him she said "I'm going to hold you to that Mr. Cole." She walked over to him while he was turned away still looking in the refrigerator and put her arms around his waist.

Just the touch of her gave him new neuro paths of joy in his nervous system. By knowing this he somehow started to remember being a medical doctor once before and this meant even more to him now. Quickly she went right in and started helping him prepare breakfast and he thought they worked well as a team very well indeed.

Talk about excitement, not only were they getting married today but last night they met her great and great-great grandparents! All of this in a dream that seemed so real and in a strange way it was real. Daisy spent the better part of the morning asking Rick to explain what that all was about last night. Even with his knowledge of quantum physics he did the best he could, but she still will need to learn more in her future dreams.

"I don't even want to ask why you've taken so long to get down here, but we've got a lot of work to do, and we have people showing up within an hour. So you two need to eat your breakfast and get ready." Brad said as he served their food with a wink.

"Grandpa I was asking Rick to explain to me the quantum physics of what happened last night." Then she gave him a surprised look and said "besides we did that before going to bed."

Gloria laughed and said "you go girl that was funny."

Both Rick and Brad laughed too, then got up went into the kitchen, and started washing the dishes while the girls finished up. It wasn't long after this that the door started knocking and getting this wedding day put together had officially begun.

Scrambling around the farm, it looked like a carnival had hit. There were trucks all over, people moving tables, chairs and, props all over the place. Daisy was still inside with Gloria putting the reception together until then they took off to her room, she was so nervous. Gloria felt so honored to be her new grandmother and to be there for her. Daisy's mom didn't do so well after her dad died in the war, she did however raise her but shortly after that she just disappeared.

Brad and Rick had it all timed, they would need an hour to get ready, and that they would work until then. Rick needed to be busy this day because he was very nervous.

The sun was now at the third hour after lunch and their guests are arriving, they are being met and seated. The official who will perform the vows had arrived from the Assembly, and is moving into position.

Then a quiet comes all around the congregation as the music begins. It is beautiful! It magically progresses as bride maids and grooms start to walk down the aisle. Everyone watches this and they are astounded by how well this is carried out. As they are up there with the Official, the flower girls walk down the aisle spreading their daisies behind them.

A hush falls over the crowd and there she appears with her grandpa. Holding his forearm she waits for him to start, staying in step as they slowly proceed down to the wedding party that awaits them. As they walked she asked him "am I doing the right thing by getting married?"

"Daisy do you love him and want to spend your life with him?"

"Yes, I do grandpa very much. Do you like him?"

"My dear that's a silly question, I think he's a wonderful man and I'm honored to give your hand to him in marriage."

As he finished saying that, there they were in front of Herthro who asked them "who gives this lady's hand in marriage?"

Brad said "I do."

Before the wedding Rick asked Seliah to help him write a poem to read to her before they would say their vows. She mostly took his information and wrote this;

My One Love

I can't help but want to tell you this
Bout' how you've made my life so bliss
Sweet and soft are words that tell
How far for you that this heart fell

This day I give you my heart
To be with yours and never part
You to be my angel each night
For courage holding the light

Deep inside this my heart so true
All I have I will share it with you
Live this life with me now and forever
While sailing through storms together

Rick sang his song to her, then Herthro read the marriage vows which they agreed upon, and then they kissed. Now the party will begin! This reception was a blast! The food was great, the wine awesome, and the band played all their favorite songs. Daisy and Rick cut the cake then Brad gave a toast, and took Daisy to the dance floor.

Once they finished their dance, Brad asked Gloria to dance, and they danced so elegantly together. Seliah smiled on the whole event and felt so complete in her new life now.

CHAPTER 17

They did not want a big wedding, so it was held on the farm, and it wasn't long until Gloria and Brad were married. Shortly after Daisy graduated and before she started law school they finished building their cottage. Moving out of town then moving into their new home only had one drawback, and that was their drive to school. The good thing about this was that they managed to carpool together and this gave them more time to communicate with each other without distractions.

Gloria and Brad were a great support team for them. They both knew that these two were working hard in school, and that they would do great things one day. The more Brad would visit the High Council in his dreams the more he would remember how much Daisy was like her great-great grandma Daanic.

It was almost uncanny how she graduated with a BA in Politics, just like her great-great grandmother Daanic, and she is now working on her Law degree. Then meeting and marrying a future doctor just like her great-great grandpa Paul. Brad did his best to explain all of this to Gloria and she thought that the whole thing was either planned or guided by someone. The one constant was these two girls and politics.

As time progressed Rick became a doctor and Daisy passed the bar. He worked at the local clinic during the week as a family doctor then every third week end he would work in the ER at the hospital. She however became a public defender for Tarmish where she would travel a few times a week for court cases or to work with her clients.

Gloria loved him so much but knew that day would come and Brad would leave his body. Over the last year he had really gone downhill and just couldn't move around like before. The one thing she was thankful for was that he didn't lose his memory at any time, if anything he was more cognizant as to what was happening than before his physical decline. During a dream a few months ago he was told that at the end of the season he would return home to the Pleiades.

His ashes were spread over the vineyards and Rick just knew that those grapes would be known as the best ones ever. Many tears were shed that day but they all looked forward to seeing him soon in their dreams. Living in their cottage for several years was wonderful but now with them talking about children Gloria encouraged them to move into the big house where there was plenty of room.

Daisy was pregnant and Gloria was so happy for her. The pub was sold a couple of years after she married Brad so Gloria was more than willing to stay at home and care for Daisy. Rick continued being a doctor while the girls took care of the farm until she was in her fourth month. That's when Rick hired a young couple that had graduated from college with degrees in agriculture. This couple would work the farm, live in the cottage, and soon become part of the family.

Funny how the things that change seem to be the same and this is so true with Daisy's life. Now knowing who her great-great grandma is makes her path in life even more interesting. With Brenda as her grandma she was influenced by her greatly and Brenda would always teach her to do what was right. When Brenda learned of Daisy's gift to do mind control this made her want to guide her even more.

The world had grown to a population of over four billion. The fact that the ones that were here first never accepted the Tres Vagans, mainly because they looked more elven, and had two small horns on their head was the Sorentito's reason for not liking them. The Sorentito people looked more reptilian, but with two arms, and walking on two legs. Hatred like this was just a few of the things that King Barborda used to keep them apart.

When the Tres Vagans arrived they were greatly outnumbered on the planet, and if the Sorentito's would have located them sooner they would have destroyed their entire civilization. Luckily they didn't and the Vagans not only grew in population, technology but also some became masters of the mind and that proved to be something the Sorentito's couldn't fight against and win.

Unfortunately or not neither side would be capable to conquer the other yet. With many attempts to try and make peace the Vagan people chose not to build war machines or have large standing armies. Opposite to this the Sorentito people did have a large military force and did not learn to be successful with farming in order to maintain a healthy supply of food for their people. A perfect example of cause and effect in that with no good food supplies, but instead only a large military, then the possibility of war will only grow.

As their three children grew up smart, strong, and very conscious of what's around them. They couldn't be happier as parents to have given them all their love those years of growing up. The youngest was finishing her last year of public education and she will then go to medical college like her dad.

In all the years spent with Gloria while raising the children, this helped Daisy to become even more powerful as a Master Vagan. Her dreams spent visiting the High Council and learning from Daanic were also instrumental in dealing with the troubles that will come to planet Earth very soon.

Rick was blessed that one of their girls became obsessed with the winery just like he was. She was the oldest and when her little brother was born, she was four at the time, and all she wanted to do was help her mom and Gloria mother him.

Their son Paul was now attending the military academy and had two more years to go. When he was young he would study the wars that had happened before and Daisy thought he might become a politician. I suppose he will follow after his grandpa's example, Daisy thought but she prays he doesn't die in a war like he did. Lots of prayers between her and Gloria are happening now that he is pursuing a military career.

In the years that followed the world continued to move onward but not necessarily in a positive way. With Cleo in college, Daisy decided to take Herthro up on his offer for her to work for him as he was still the High Councilor, and Daisy was being pushed by Gloria to join him now that the children were grown.

Her first day in the Assembly and she is more than ready to start learning. Meeting her at the steps was one of Herthro's aides, who seeing her walk up the steps asked "you must be Daisy Brackett?"

"Why yes I am, and are you part of the High Councilor Herthro's staff?"

"Yes mam, I'm a summer intern. Now would you follow me please?"

Entering into his large chamber she remembered the day when it was her grandma's. That was a long time ago and she was very pleased with the way Herthro took over after she passed. He was excited to have her there and he knew that one day this job will be hers.   Brenda would tell him that Daisy was a special girl and that after a life of raising children she will return to politics. Somehow Brenda knew how her life would progress even when she wasn't there to directly influence it.

He was always a fan of Daisy, especially when she was working with Gloria, and the other Master Vagans. As she entered, he greeted her and said "welcome Daisy, I'm so glad you are here, take the rest of the day to have your things brought in, and then take your time getting settled. We can have dinner tonight around seven and I'll send my car here to pick you up."

"Thank you, Your Honor that will be fine."

That's just what she did and it did take some time to unpack all the books that her grandma left her. Her title is not just an aide to the High Councilor, she is his assistant and second in command!

Sitting in her chair behind this big wooden desk, she looked at the pictures that were placed on her wall. All of them put everything in perspective because they are ones of her wedding day, several of her children, one of her grandpa's wedding to Gloria, and then the one of Brenda in her outfit as the High Councilor.

Time passed by very quickly and before she could blink the long black car pulled up. The driver parked, Herthro went inside to her chamber, and knocked on the door. Opening the door Daisy smiled and said "please come in."

"Okay but we only have a few minutes."

"As you wish, then I'm ready to go."

Into the car she entered and sat across from him. They both talked about almost everything that had transpired in their lives with them in the last twenty years. What a joyous ride to the restaurant they had these two people with one powerfully beautiful person in common.

Pulling up he said "it's so good to have you here and I now feel Brenda has returned to her place through you."

"Thank you Your Grace you are so gracious."

Before they went to exit the car he said to the driver "give us several minutes before we leave the vehicle please."

"Yes, Your Honor just let me know when you are ready."

He then turned to look at Daisy and said "let's take some time to breathe in all the energy that we've created remembering your grandma and my very close friend. Shall we just meditate on that concept before having dinner?"

"With pleasure, Your Honor" and then she breathed in deep and deliberately she began her meditation.

The time was momentarily frozen and the air was cool as he let the windows down a few inches. They both could feel the energy around them and it was like magic to behold this feeling. Herthro and Daisy knew that Brenda was there with them this evening. He opened his eyes and said "are you ready?"

"Sure Your Honor let's go eat, I don't want to arrive home too late."

"I'll make sure you get home at a reasonable hour. Did you let Rick know you will be late?"

"Yes, I told him we were having dinner."

Out of the car and into the restaurant they went. He talked with her about the way things were shaping up with the people of Sorentito and how it's becoming almost impossible to keep them at bay. They talked about what kind of solutions could be offered. They were brought down one by one with an ever depressing reality of how unresponsive the enemy can be to reason with.

This dinner was not as pleasant as they wished it would have been, but these things needed to be discussed. Quite impressive are her abilities to deal with situations that need an uncommon energy, very few possess, and none at the levels she has. The evening ended and she was driven home and would return back to the Assembly in three days.

Gloria was so happy that Daisy was now in the Assembly and she promised Brenda that she would help get her in there when the time was right. Twenty-one years raising children with Gloria while they both perfected the skills of being a Vagan Master. During this time they kept some connections with their former group of masters.

This week end was planned months ago when the last child was still at home. Now that she has gone to college they will take a small vacation. Daisy had scheduled these days with Herthro before starting in the Assembly. Rick wasn't pulling hospital duty this week end and Daisy wasn't going to the Assembly for a few days.

Gloria walked into the living room and noticed them both on the couch. She clapped her hands and said "are you two packed and ready for your vacation?"

They both jumped up and Daisy said "Gloria! You about gave me a heart attack."

'Well are you two ready for your vacation?"

Rick laughed and said "I guess not because I haven't packed yet."

"I suggest we get that done because we need to leave in an hour if you plan on catching your flight."

Always there to keep these two very busy people on track, and then to make sure they are taken care of, is what Gloria does. She dropped them off at the airport, they got through security and then they were off to the islands for some R and R. It was so wonderful that they could spend this time together to reconnect, because Daisy and Rick have a love that will continue through time.

They enjoyed their time on the island, down on the beach swimming, and drinking those drinks that come with little umbrellas. Daisy was reading the newspaper on her table and read an article of how bad things were for Tarmish. She read how their crops were not bringing in the yield needed to feed the people, but not wanting to ruin their vacation she kept this information to herself.

"Rick look, parachute rides, let's do that."

He was surprised and said "are you sure I thought you were afraid of heights?"

"I need to face all my fears and this is a way to conquer that one."

"Okay then let's go!"

Thoughts racing through her mind about how high those parachutes were and she then worried about what she'd gotten herself into. "Not today, not today," she told herself, "I'm going to be brave."

Stepping up in line they were next and Rick looked at her and said "we can turn around if you want to?"

"What, and miss this opportunity to conquer one of my fears? I want to do this and I will do this."

The man told her to lift her arms so he could put the harness over her. She never thought her arms weighed five hundred pounds each, it was so hard to keep them up there. Rick was all ready and he yelled out to her over the boats engine noise "this is going to be great!"

They went higher and higher until they reached the peak. She held on tight, then when her chute climbed up no more, her eyes opened up. Looking down was a shock to her and then over the water she tried to catch her balance. Rick was just looking around and enjoying the view from up there. Finally after a few minutes the fear of heights started to leave her, she began to enjoy the ride, and yelled over to Rick "this is great!"

He was too far away to hear her, but seeing the smile on her face, he just gave her two thumbs up instead. The boat started to slow down and their chutes began to slowly travel back to the water. Never in a parachute before caused them to have a difficult time landing in the water. It was only about five feet deep where the boat swung them around to land. Then helpers showed up and released them from the harnesses.

The first thing she did after they were freed was to run over to him, and give him a big hug and a kiss. Rick was excited too and picked her up and said "do you want to do it again!"

"I do, but let's take a break first."

Lovebirds they will always be and this short vacation was so needed for them. After all the problems they have been through, this was a wonderful time spent for them.

While they were away Gloria and Herthro spent the weekend in the city and this wasn't a secret meet up. No, this was to discuss the plans for Daisy's future, and these plans were in the works since she was in high school. And now they were ready to carry them forward, only these two will know what they are planning, and it will be hard to keep it a secret.

Showing up at this high end hotel and convention center was Gloria with her bags in tow. Herthro had already had his room secured and all his luggage put in there. Then walking up to the front desk to get her keys and to leave a credit card, Gloria was surprised when the clerk said "we won't need your card, the room and all your expenses are complimentary because you are the guest of the High Councilor."

The meeting went off without a hitch, the main topic they talked about was Daisy's ascension to become the next High Councilor, and soon. This was something that they made plans for and rehearsed on how they were going to present this to her. It wasn't that they didn't feel Daisy would want to become this, they just weren't sure if she would agree to take over so quickly.

CHAPTER 18

War! That's what has happened and it's a full scale one. This time there was no stopping it, the harvest in Tarmish and other places around the world of the Vagan people was dire. Only Otium as a large community of people was able to put enough away for the winter. Usually most of Sorentito's people were always in short supply and they could count on the good nature of others particularly the Vagan people for help.

Now they did their best to help but there just wasn't enough food to solve the world's problem this time. King Barborda had died and his son took over the throne. Now this young king knew very little and there certainly was little he could have learned from his dad. The world is in a lot of trouble now and it will take someone with an overwhelming amount of courage to resolve it.

Daisy is now the High Councilor and one of the first things she did was to travel across the Tres Vagan world. In doing this she was able to gather a lot of knowledge that would be useful in the future. Places that were suffering from a lack of education were given a group of Master Vagans to help guide their current educators. If an area had problems with food supplies, that need would be addressed by the Master Vagans too.

All in all she did an excellent job of using these Masters to help bring the Tres Vagan kingdom up to where all areas were prosperous. Then this horrible drought came and now several years later it hasn't changed. Some of Daisy's Engineers wanted to build large irrigation canals to direct some water from the ice caps. Although this idea was shown that if accomplished it would only bring temporary relief and in the end destroy much of the artic. The Scientist proved that this would then throw things out of balance, and that it would be nearly a century before the planet's weather stabilized again.

But after a few years they were outvoted and the Engineers started building the canals. The problem was that this project will take two more years before any water will flow. Already seven years into the drought and having to wait two more years was way too long for the world. Also the Sorentito people were told by their king that the drought was the Tres Vagans fault.

Their cities were attacked by a full scale assault force and that was something many of them couldn't withstand. From an advantage point in the sky, Daisy used satellite images to map out the enemy's battle locations. With this she devised a plan to evacuate her people at the first sign of an invasion. Only the military will stay back to hold off the attackers and in doing so allow her people to escape further away from danger.

Tarmish is being bombarded with heavy mortar shells, but they were prepared for this. Underground bunkers were built months ago and the citizens are now down below and safe. Her son Paul is part of the Calvary unit that flew down to help hold them off with small aircraft and maneuvers designed to slow down the enemy. Paul is a Major and he is a commander of one of the air squadrons.

Part of the plan was to allow the Sorentito's to capture the cities, but to weaken their military along the way, thus leaving their homes behind. The enemy had no choice but to press forward when those cities fell. The Vagans would hold them off long enough to have their people escape into the next town. In that town all of the homes would take in the fleeing families. Single people would bunk at the local gyms and motels, if there were no rooms left in the homes.

Receiving word from the general, who was in charge of the evacuation, and the battle of Tarmish, she gave her report to Daisy. In the report she was informed that her son Paul was safe and on his way back to Otium. The army of Sorentito would now move into Tarmish and find some food and supplies there. However, they did not find enough to take back home to their people. Then just a few of the enemy's military men would realize that it was strange that any supplies would be left, and that this might be part of Daisy's plan.

This same thing would occur around the world. Daisy's Vagan people would put up a fight, to keep the attackers from taking over the cities, until their people escaped to the next one. Needless to say the Engineers are not digging a pipeline from the Artic to bring water down. Time and again while the enemy is attacking Daisy has her people reorganizing into a larger force each time they moved back.

With winter getting worse, the enemy can't move forward or backwards, and they are stuck in the cities that they conquered. They're starting to get very low on fuel and supplies and any fuel they do have needs to be rationed for heat only. All the while Daisy has several large teams of all types of her people that have travelled to the home cities of the enemy.

With the armies of the Sorentito's stuck in many cities around the northern hemisphere there are none left to protect their homes that they left unguarded. While King Fredric didn't think that the Tres Vagan people would consider attacking their cities, he was more concerned with conquering with his military. That said, Daisy's people didn't attack, but what they did do was to show them mercy and enter in to help the women and the children. They brought plenty of food and supplies with them to accomplish this.

Twice a week planes would fly by the captured cities and at first the Sorentito army would shoot at them, but luckily none of them were shot down or the Vagan people would really be angry. Funny thing was that after the planes left, these packages that were dropped were brought inside the city, some of the soldiers would shoot at them, and then later go with a bomb squad and try to defuse them. They felt pretty stupid when it was learned that the first few packages they destroyed were filled with food and water.

Even the enemy got a good laugh out of that one, and some would say something like "it's a good thing they didn't send us cooking fuels or we would have thought they really were bombs! The packages were measured to be enough to sustain them through the winter and nothing more. This sign of good faith would have an even greater positive effect later.

Some of the enemy cities that were close to any Vagan ones would start the process of becoming one united people. There were some standouts and Daisy knew this would happen. She decided the best thing would be to just continue to help them and it will all work itself out in time. By the end of the winter most of the enemy cities in the northern hemisphere had joined with the Vagan people.

Soon the winter was coming to an end and the supply drops were starting to become larger. This made a lot of the enemy think, do they want to attack the good people that kept them alive during the winter, or do they take what supplies they can home to their people? These questions caused a lot of frustrations for King Fredric and his henchmen. They had more problems than they could handle, to the point that any attacks on the Vagan people were small, and weak, that they put them down quickly, and mostly by just mental suggestions from the Vagan Masters.

As the spring weather came the people of Sorentito that joined with the Vagans wanted to call themselves Vagans. Daisy was honored but thought that it would be best if they came up with a name for them all to be used. Looking through the books of the laws from Millennia she came across one from the old Earth.

This new name she found was "humans", this word was something that not only brought them together, but it came from the word humanity, which also encompassed another word humane. Humane spelled it all out so clearly, because it means to help one another, and this war was won by doing just that. So their new name and moto is "we are human because we are humane."

Herthro asked to talk with Daisy after she returned to Otium. He had long retired, and wasn't the man he used to be, but he did still have his mind intact. When she arrived he greeted her in his wheel chair and told her how proud he was of her accomplishments. There was one thing that he had wanted to ask her, and he finally did when he said "Daisy was the food supply of our people really low or did you just manufacture that to incite a war?"

"My friend and mentor I can't tell anyone that for sure, it would be like being a great poker player and giving away my bluffs. I will however tell you this..."

This was not said in just, she really couldn't tell anyone her secret, because too many people had to die to bring this constant cycle of war, and terror that the kings of the Sorentito people brought all these hundreds of years. Even with all that was gained Daisy was still very sad from all the lost lives in this war.

Grandma Seliah and great-great grandma Daanic both looked upon their sweet girl, who took on the evil in her world, and defeated it with kindness and mercy. So they wrote this song to remember her triumph.

Daisy's Way

Seeming to have it all she will be
All she has is given away you see
In her heart she knows all are the same
By looks and location give each a name

This is not the way to live she cries out
Love each as one is what life is about
When some were in need she made a way
That the people loved her enough to say

She is loved but finds herself so alone
Striving to make sure all have a home
We know that her time there has a limit
For she will be here and not to dream it

So this is Daisy's way
To give love each day
Yes Daisy's way
Bright as a ray

King Fredric and his loyal subjects went back to their kingdom. Daisy instructed her people to help the guards that the king left behind to secure the palace. Usually in history a former king's subjects will move in and take all they can and leave the place destroyed. Not this time because part of her grand plan included a transfer of power.

All around the northern hemisphere, King Frederic's empire fell, while the people celebrated their new freedoms. If these people were leaders or women that couldn't join the King's government, they were now allowed to join the new Human one. If the women had leadership qualities, studied civics or had a desire to join then there was a path for them to achieve their goals. The men that were currently in the King's government were vetted and held to pay for their crimes.

As King Fredric returned with his guards he was welcomed by the High Councilor. Knowing that he wouldn't talk with her before unless he was trying to deceive her, then why did he receive this welcome from her? Now that he has been defeated one would think why would she give him the time of day? Well Daisy is a different type of leader, because she will not return evil for evil, his palace was left intact, and they will meet there for the next three days.

While the two of them were alone in their meeting, he asked her "why are you being so kind to me?"

Looking him squarely in the eyes she said "your Majesty there is no reason to not show you respect."

He didn't even know what to say as he sat there just too dumbfounded to speak. This meeting was at first very uncomfortable for him because he was waiting to be judged for all his crimes. His crimes were listed and he was told that restitution needed to be made. He wasn't held accountable for his father's crimes and payment was already made to the people that were harmed.

During this meeting King Fredric did try and get some military secrets from her. Although it wasn't that she didn't tell him everything, she did, his problem was not being able to comprehend it. To his surprise she had one of her aides bring in a large document that she took and sat it down between them. Then he said "what is this?"

"Well your Majesty, it's an agreement I would like to go over with you."

"An agreement to what, this can't be a surrender paper I've already signed that one?"

"No, it's not that, it is an agreement that I offer you to help you keep a kingdom in the southern hemisphere."

A surprised look and then he was eager to discuss this. He then said "so I can stay in power?"

'Yes, you will be one of seven kings in each of the seven continents that report to me."

This new turn of events was very interesting to him. Daisy had done her homework and found a large area in South America where the people still were loyal to the king. This time when he returns he will still be their king but his rule will fall under the laws of the Human government. She then went over all the laws and freedoms that his people will have that they didn't before.

It is the last day, the day before was a doozy for the king, he spent a lot of time reading, and learning all the new laws while

Daisy tested him, and made sure he understood them all. This king will be mostly a figurehead and with a group of Vagan Masters living nearby to monitor him from afar. A final handshake first then he gave her a hug and said "thank you Your Grace you are a special human being and I won't let you down."

There was nothing else for her to say, she just waved goodbye to all of her kings and queens. Now the first order of business will be for her to travel the world, set up these remaining six queens and kings in their new kingdoms. Rick asked her during their travel to Asia "why do you set them up as queens and kings and not elected officials?"

"That's because an elected official will be constantly running for office."

"So how does putting someone permanent over them make it better? What if this queen or king is a terrible leader and rules their people wrongly?"

"Simple they will be replaced because they know the laws that they have to abide by."

"How will you know if they are breaking the laws?"

"We are stationing Vagan Masters near each palace."

There were many pockets of resistance around the world. Most were very small, and handled without a lot of trouble. For the most part the world was peaceful, the people are now one, and they can control their own futures.

In one of the kingdoms Daisy was called to settle a problem the Sorentito people had. It was Queen Marsha who summoned her to come there, because neither she nor the Master Vagans could find anything in the law that dealt with their current situation. This was in the continent of North America where the Vagans haven't been in many years. The settlement that was there before was conquered hundreds of years ago and the Vagan people were made to be slaves until they slowly died out.

On her way there she was given all the information and therefore started to put a speech together. She felt that there didn't need to be laws on how humans lived, as long as they don't cause any harm to others. One thing she requested was an announcement that in two days there will be a proclamation read by her the High Councilor.

When she arrived she immediately went into action to put a stop to this hatred and no violence was used to do that. She learned that in most cases just a show of support backed with force worked. Now this didn't immediately change their minds or hearts, whichever one was out of whack it didn't matter, it would be changed soon.

After the rule of King Barborda and then King Fredric these Sorentito people were a mess, especially the men. Trying to talk to them and explain that how they felt about others was wrong wasn't well accepted. For the next two days Daisy would spend many hours going over in her mind and on her tablet the speech she needed to give. Then after two days she was ready and Queen Marsha had the royal palace prepared for this day.

The Queen was announced and then she walked up to the podium and said *"my fellow North Americans this is a very special day for with us today is Her Grace High Councilor Daisy. So please welcome her and then listen to what she has to say. Thank you all and thank you Your Grace."*

With a big hug from Marsha, Daisy then turned around to speak. This is what she said *"you have a very different history than the rest of the world. Hundreds of years ago the settlers of the Tres Vagans were captured by the then Sorentito people here in North America and from our history this was a terrible time for*

North America. If you don't know the rest of the story you can research it later. Why I decided to come here today was to try to bring some understanding of what it means to be a new common people known as humans..."

She paused because there was a lot of cheering and applause and once they stopped she continued and said *"thank you for that, we should all be free to celebrate our new name of human, for it is now a people that are together as one. As far as any laws about if some should be allowed to fall in love or not because they are from a different heritage is absurd."*

They were then quiet and mostly some from fear of others until Daisy picked up on this and said *"this cannot be tolerated, we are now one people, diversity needs to be embraced, and celebrated too, but not used to separate us. Never do we want to force someone to think or feel a certain way, however we do encourage them to open up their hearts and see that this is a beautiful thing. The trick is to join in and then ride the river with the rest of us as one."*

Another loud applause which lasted for only a few minutes, and Daisy said *"Thank you again, now let's not let our feelings cause us to do things that are hateful. Remember our name is human which is linked to being humane to others. If you don't like another human, maybe you disagree with how they exercise their freedoms, this is not against the law until you act on your dislikes, and hurt another. I would like to come back here again and find that this continent has become an example on how people can be free and get along."*

She stood back and took a drink of water then returned and said *"are there any questions?"* Looking into the crowd they all seemed to understand and asked no questions. Then she just turned and walked away.

Queen Marsha stood behind the podium and thanked Daisy and bid her farewell.

Daisy had one more stop before returning to Europe and the city of Otium. This stop would be in South America and it involved equal rights for all adults to marry each other. She didn't use the same speech but it was very similar and only the history of the continent was not mentioned. The best part of her speech was how she gave examples of how we are all different and that each has a beautiful sound to add to this song we are creating.

The King Was very impressed and honored to have her there. Also during her visit they talked about equal rights for women because this used to be mostly a Sorentito area. Now women can go to all the schools and also be a part of the government.

Daisy returned home and during a dream she visited the High Council. There Daanic listened to her tell her grandma Seliah about her travels around the world and how she was able to set up several new kingdoms that were under her control. The one thing that impressed Daanic the most was the way the whole world took on the name of human, and how under this name they became one people.

During her dream Daanic or Seliah she couldn't remember which one had given her this song. This morning she took Rick by the hand a walked him down to the lake. There she settled into the gazebo, took her tablet out, and wrote down the song she was given. After writing it she laid back and closed her eyes and said "Rick I finished the song from last night."

"Wonderful, please sing it to me."

Human

Yes we look different and we are afraid.
Living our lives as one people was dear.
Happier days they were without drama.
Until these different people landed here

Their ways were strange and scared us.
Look at them see they even have a tail.
They then used some type of dark magic.
So our plants that grew food would fail.

Humans are flawed and destined to fear.
If something is new and not made clear.

Knowing that they are the enemy is true.
They built their settlements on our land.
They were strong so we became mighty.
To defend ourselves here we will stand.

Seeing their plans could destroy us all.
Our new army was needed to stop that.
We attacked first to stop these invaders.
Then we conquered them in nothing flat.

Humans then turn all fear into hate.
Harming their neighbors it's too late.

War ended with both sides holding on.
Their cities are ours now to become.
What we wanted was to stop their ways.
After a cold winter then we were done.

Our towns needed food, water, and heat.
Planes flew by and dropped supplies.
First we thought they might be bombs.
Their kindness came down from the skies.

Humans follow hate to an end.
Love comes in like Angels wind.

People are shown what laws do.
Healing is all in the air this day
Wrongs are to be righted justly.
Forgiving them is the only way.

All come together to now be one.
Duality doesn't end on any day.
There is no good without bad.
The new people follow the way.

Humans can now become one.
All are human under the sun.

CHAPTER 19

With the Earth running smoothly now that Daisy is the leader. Our focus turns to Millennia, and the High Council of the Pleiades. Tamla has been the High Councilor of Millennia since her mom Margo left to become the High Councilor of the Pleiades. There Margo received her new name Daanic.

The planet Millennia was working nearly perfect and all the inhabitants are working in a profession or skill that they love to do. Even the sea life and dragons of the mountains are a part of everyday life. Some dolphins would encourage the elven people to use the spell to become one with them from time to time. These dolphins loved walking around in human form, for a change of pace.

Dragons in all the different mountain ranges had a thriving business of rides and mining minerals. Shasha was in charge of the infrastructure because for some reason she had a love for bridges and roads. A plan was put together by her to use limited amounts of the planet for movement. No roads touched the ground, because the vehicles were made with an anti-gravity magnetic force that kept them in the air.

Daisy started travelling to Millennia in her sleep along with many of the Vagan Masters and a select few of other humans. They would meet with her to discuss what happens on Millennia in governing the people. This was beneficial to her with all the new changes coming on Earth with the new world government.

Once in a while they would travel to the Pleiades and visit Daanic and Seliah and occasionally they would be visited by Jillela and Ella but this was rare. When Daisy visited the Pleiades she would request to spend time with great-great grandpa Paul, sometimes they would shoot over to the moon, and visit Amerorth.

This was how it all went for quite some time now on Millennia and on Earth. Daisy would learn so much and seeing her dad on Millennia was very special since she was so young when he died in the war. These astral dream visits left Daisy looking forward to the day when she would travel to Millennia for the last time.

All the information Daisy passed on to Earth that she learned from Millennia and the Pleiades made for a lot of good changes. Later the humans started calling themselves by the continent they were from except for the Master Vagans and the High Councilor. They would continue to only think of themselves as humans.

Maj. Paul Brackett made General and was in charge of the United World forces that were created only to keep the peace. Rick still was a doctor and had a whole wing at the Otium Heart Center. Daisy shared with him some of the information that her grandparents put together while they were Cardiologists on Millennia by studying the data from the first Earth age.

Shortly after the big world war Gloria left her body, went to the Pleiades to be on Seliah's staff, and then her name was changed to Uriah. When Herthro left he quickly volunteered and returned to Earth, but no one knows who he is now. Many times before when people would leave Earth not many knew where they then would go.

King Fredric became a very loyal assistant to Daisy and he ruled as a benevolent king. Anytime Daisy would visit him she could always feel the love from his people of South America. Even King Fredric tells the story of the coup that Daisy pulled off to end the wars on Earth. This was also written in the military tactics lessons that are taught at all the military academies on Earth.

In the world the people did start to separate themselves again, some by the boundaries that they had and others still mostly by the differences of colour. Time and time she would try and address this but there were always a small group that held on to a belief that they were better than others because of these differences. No matter at what cost it would be, there can't be another world war, and that was simply the final word from Daisy.

Things were slowly starting to revert back to the way they were before the war. One place that she would see occasionally was Tarmish it seemed that there was a growing number of people that wanted to take short cuts with farming and taking care of the land. Over time the Master Vagan numbers slowly dwindled and not many new people had that power or wanted to learn it anymore.

Daisy was growing more and more tired trying to prevent the world from falling back into the old ways. In some places the people were requesting that their leaders do more for them, because they wanted to have more leisure time. By studying the first Earth age with the problems they encountered she tried to warn them and direct their leaders to solve these problems. But the pressure from the people caused some leaders to cave in and that's when the decline began to spiral out of control.

Talking with her grandma Seliah, she didn't understand her when she said that all these things are meant to happen. With that logic Daisy asked her "why do we even try to make things better then?"

Seliah then told her that "it's just the way of the universe" and when she goes back to the Source she will understand.

One more thing that Seliah left her with was encouragement to just keep trying and she'll save some people.

Although armed with this new information, this didn't make Daisy feel any better. Just the knowledge that things will happen the way they are supposed to. Nothing she can do will change the course of events of the world but there are many people she will reach in doing what's right. Not to mention she has her family to look out for also.

Some call it a harvest of souls, but others say that humans are only slaves for some aliens to mine the Earth's materials for them. Over time when the world benefited without war for decades the people used this freedom to invent great things. With freedom comes responsibility and Daisy tried to guide many people not to follow the ones that started or believed in crazy conspiracies.

Through these conspiracies came new religions that differed greatly from the ones already established. These new religions targeted the people that just couldn't seem to become part of the current prosperity that had inhabited the planet. Although they weren't targeted by these fringe religions, there were some very wealthy people that joined them with the intent of buying their way up their leadership levels.

One of those was a prior high ranking member from the former King Fredric's reign. He just couldn't agree with the new freedoms given to women and really didn't like any type of mixed marriages. Then there were many who didn't like the growing prosperity gap and Daisy was in league with them on that issue. So yes, there were some issues that did need to be fixed, but the problem was that most religious leaders would use some misunderstood idea of a god to mobilize the disenfranchised people.

"This just can't be real" Daisy cried out to the universe while she stood next to her gazebo by the lake. Pondering what she had been told by her family up in the clouds and then seeing it all unfold each day was discouraging. Not that she questions her grandma Seliah, or that the history written isn't there as a pattern. What bothered her was that she didn't feel connected to the people of Earth anymore.

Going through the motions, doing less and less each time, this was a disturbing thing. Watching groups of people separate from the rest and base this on religious grounds. She felt she could do nothing to stop them and in many causes they did have a good reason to leave. Wanting them to stay to work it out and make it better were just words with no backing. With very few Master Vagans left in the world, peace started to break down and some cities even fell apart.

All these thoughts captivated her heart and mind. She knew what to do so she started to chant an old familiar yoga mantra and after several minutes she went into the awakening of her Kundalini. Then minutes spent in this bliss as the Kundalini moved up her spine to reach within the Sahasrara Chakra at the top of her head, she wrote this song;

Moving Upward

To fight for peace sounds like a contradiction
Knowing the true goal even from its inception
So people become richer and others remain poor
Seeing the riches of this world has plenty in store

Maybe they're right we are merely slaves to mine
All the minerals for others and to them that is fine
Become a Master and use your power to guide all
Being aware that day will come to answer the call

All this is Moving Upward right or wrong
All this is Moving Upward to sing this song
Many will separate from you and not want to share
Controlling their heart with their mind to not care

It's easy so easy to be a judge of the good and bad
This is so true but don't get caught in this to be sad
Let the Spirit fly and join the ones above the clouds
From the chaos and confusion amongst the crowds

Open your heart to learn on this path of ascension
Blessing to all while on the earthly plan of remission
All this is Moving Upward right or wrong
All this is Moving Upward to sing this song

This was her first song and it seems she had a talent given to her from two other people. Rick thought it was beautiful and really conveyed a positive message.

North America started to revert to their old ways once again and Daisy couldn't seem to stop them. Poor Queen Marsha worked so hard to convince them that this wasn't the way to go, but over time those people wouldn't listen. First a series of elections happened and little by little they would get their people elected. Then the day arrived that they had enough votes to influence legislation and this one was a doozy. They had proposed to pull out of the World Human Government because they claimed that they were giving more to support it than most of the world did.

Daisy did know what was going on and for several years she poured in resources there to try and turn the tide. One thing she couldn't deny was that this river was flowing in one direction and she wasn't going to change it. This vote was shelved until now and although it didn't pass it did cause for there to be riots in the streets of some North American cities. The proposal not passing gave Daisy some well needed time to devise a plan before it came up for a vote on the next docket.

What Daisy was able to do was to negotiate with this new party called "Sorentito" to honor their heritage. In doing so she was able to safely pull out the current Vagan people and any others who felt that they were Humans. This situation was getting tense and Daisy feared they would go after Queen Marsha soon. The new leader named Jerod made himself the new king and celebrated winning back North America without a shot.

As with most dictators you can't trust them to keep their agreements. King Jerod amassed a very large army and started to move on the palace that the queen was in. She had been given two weeks to vacate, but King Jerod wanted her out now and wanted to keep her people there as slaves. This would make part of their conspiracy correct in that there would be slaves on Earth.

Moving very quickly, Daisy needed to get reinforcements in there fast, she called on her son General Paul for help, he had an idea and she had no choice but to let him do it. Information was coming in while General Paul starting calling his commanders to get ready with operation "Save the Queen."

Seeing what was coming Queen Marsha sent her army out to intercept King Jerod's. Word came in through a secure line from Daisy that Marsha just needed to give her 18 hours to have a force there. During that time she was told to gather up all her people and to get them behind their lines for safety.

Fighting began several hours after the lines formed outside the palace. Before that, the cities were a mass of chaos, where Jerod's people were grouping together, while Marsha's were escaping, and heading for the palace. During this time Jerod's people had no command structure therefore Marsha's weren't in danger yet. Then he showed up with his army and gathered the others that were grouping together. That's when they started chasing after Marsha's people fleeing for the palace and she sent out the Calvary to bring them in quickly. There were some casualties but nothing substantial and most of the people made it to safety.

The enemy's size was growing larger by the minute and Marsha could feel the pressure of their impending attack. Remembering what Daisy instructed her to do so her army was placed in lines one behind the other. Looking at the numbers she wasn't confident that they could hold them off long enough for the reinforcements to arrive. Later she went to the front lines to give all her soldiers courage to do their job.

Returning to the palace to carry out the plan given to her by Daisy, Marsha was very worried about her people's safety. Then after a couple of hours, word came that the battle had begun. The first line held for almost half an hour and then retreated back to the second line some four hundred kilometers away, they retreated before they could possibly be overrun. There

Marsha's army regrouped while Jerod's took up positions in their newly conquered territory.

Losing ground would cause many leaders to worry but Marsha could now see how this plan was working. New supplies were sent to the newly formed front line and all injured were brought back to the infirmary. Feeling like the conqueror, Jerod sent word up to the front that they would attack in half an hour, and so he sent more troops up there.

Knowing that war is never the answer, Daisy felt that this plan of slowing the enemy down while evacuating her people was the best thing to do for now. Seeing Jerod's army start another volley of mortar fire on the frontline, she gave the order to fire back, and to hold the line for forty-five minutes.

The mortar fire lasted for almost twenty-five minutes and then sensing that their enemy's lines were weakened Jerod's men prepared to attack. Coming out of their safe bunkers Marsha's soldiers formed into their fighting positions and prepared to slow down this attack.

Jerod's men moved toward the frontline shooting and screaming. Marsha's army returned fire and began their retreat at the same time. Jerod's army was not wise to what was happening, and by the time Jerod's army arrived at the frontline, Marsha's soldiers were about five kilometers away.

Jerod received word about another victory and laughed, then said to his generals "this is so easy, we'll have the palace before the morning."

Just then Marsha received word from General Paul that he and his army will be there within two hours. This gave her more hope to then send reinforcements to the newly formed line and bring back the few injured to the infirmary. Now she just needed to wait for General Paul to arrive with his army and the rescue aircraft, but Jerod's army took the airport before she knew that it had fallen.

Being farther away from their last conquered territory it took a little longer for Jerod to bring in reinforcements. He was now ready to attack again only an hour after taking the last position, while General Paul's army was still on the way there. Almost a textbook battle again, where they would move to attack, and Marsha's soldiers would slow them down while they retreated back to the next line.

Only this time when Marsha's soldiers retreated they were taking up new positions around large aircraft that had just landed. All of Marsha's people were loading onto the planes and preparing to leave. When the area in front was left open for Jerod's men to move in, the new front line was now filled with General Paul's paratroopers, they had recently jumped in behind the frontlines. They were not just soldiers they were highly trained ones with expertise in extraction and rescue missions.

Queen Marsha boarded her plane after the other aircraft starting taking off. One after another they went up into the sky headed for Europe. Once it was established that they were safely on their way, General Paul's army quickly cut off Jerod's supply lines. Paul's soldiers outflanked Jerod's main force and separated the other two. During these aggressive maneuvers Jarod became confused and didn't know what to do.

With his army split in multiple lines, surrounded with all supply and communication lines cut off, Jerod was now all but defeated. The only problem was that General Paul's army wasn't big enough to defeat Jerod's, so he just used some highly skilled precision maneuvers, that caused Jerod's army to become discombobulated.

Knowing this was the objective, Paul also had a plan to escape after this happened. With his army together and close to their aircraft, Paul then gave the order to set off the charges that were placed in strategic locations. The sounds were amazing, Jarod's men were scrambling everywhere, and then with the smoke blocking their line of sight Paul's army escaped.

Her son was successful, now on his way home, and this mother couldn't be more happy or proud. Landing at Otium airport was this amazing group of soldiers, who were cheered by a large welcoming crowd. This crowd was mostly the people from North America and then their family members. Her Grace was certainly there to award medals for these brave people even though they were only doing what they were trained for.

Having read about this kind of uprising before, Daisy thought it wise to slowly, and quietly start moving Marsha's people out from the surrounding area of King Jerod's rule. In time Marsha will have the majority of her people settled in Greenland with the thought that King Jerod will not want that land anyway. Plus it will be easier to defend from an invasion since this island was close to Europe.

This took almost a year to get them to Greenland and Jerod's kingdom covered the rest of North America. Only at the newly built canal in Panama were the borders drawn. There were several attempts to overthrow the Panama canal but every time they were repelled convincingly. After the third try Jerod decided to just leave it the way it was for now.

The original people brought to Otium with Queen Marsha were offered the choice to move to Greenland with their people. Some stayed but most went with the queen to start a new country. For the most part this island was left alone and now it was being settled by a people that wanted to do things differently. Here Queen Marsha used a lot of what she learned in Otium about caring for their surroundings and not trying to build or destroy it just for their pleasures.

Tonight Daisy will visit her great grandmothers on Millennia and to always learn something new. Falling asleep quickly, she was very tired from all of the recent events. After she traveled to Millennia, she said "so you two, what are we doing tonight?"

Tamla answered her and said "well dear you and Rick are going to pick out your home."

"Pick out our home does that mean we are dead on Earth?"

Then Rick walked up with Shasha and he said "I hope not! There are things we should take care of before that happens."

Tamla smiled and said "you are not dead and I would advise you to do just what Rick said when you awake. You never know the day or the hour but you will know when it's near."

Shasha and Tamla thought about Daisy and Rick's will, and remembered when they did the same. Daisy picked out a very nice home for her and Rick, it had a rather large lake behind their home. She asked them what jobs they will do when they arrived there again for good. Shasha explained that it would depend on what they pick out before leaving. They were told that they will start traveling there once a week to and start their preparations for this move.

The world is starting to slowly fall apart and now Daisy is being told that she will leave there soon. Although she hasn't been given the day or the hour, it was let out that it would be within a year. At the breakfast table they realized that, they were two people who had lived such beautifully chaotic lives on Earth together. Now they are being told to prepare to leave within a year, but it could be tomorrow, they don't know.

Rick poured some strong coffee and said "can you take off this week so we can start getting things in order?"

"I guess I'll have too, we don't have any choice. This information was given so let's make the most of it."

Two days later they did just that, both met with lawyers and others to make sure they're deaths will not leave anyone in the dark. This was easy to do because they had already discussed it with their children so they knew who would get what.

One thing they did do many years ago was to buy some land next to them. This land was bought with only one purpose and that was to parcel it out to their children. Each one built a beautiful home so that was taken care of. Their eldest took over the winery years ago and Rick can come in to help her whenever he feels like it. Rick learned that with his schedule as a doctor and head of a hospital wing he just couldn't maintain it alone anymore.

The most important thing for Daisy was to find her replacement and she wasn't going to wait until she died. Dr. Rick Brackett had a couple of assistants working for him so he is very confident that the hospital will pick the right one. Not to fear Daisy did have someone in mind and this person might not be a relative.

Having their financials and all put in order their Lawyer advised them to not worry about that anymore. This Lawyer was very smart she knew how to set everything up for any circumstance that could arise. At the Assembly Daisy called on her team to help her brainstorm to find her replacement.

First order of business was to gather her team and travel to the coast and relax. She had her own list and with the team together she started to pare the list down. Waiting for them to settle in she requested that they meditate and achieve Kundalini before beginning. With the soft ocean breeze blowing the trees, it then moved their Spirits all around and through them.

Deep breathing and the warm wind blowing in she had achieved the level she was looking for. Giving some others in the group a little more time she patiently waited for them while looking over her list. All eyes are open and she reads from the list "first one I have is General Paul my son."

Then she hears someone say "I didn't know he was interested in becoming the High Councilor, he would be a great one."

Daisy chuckled and said "I know, and he's even told me that he's not interested in the position."

Another aide asked her "then should we strike him off the list?"

"No, not yet, let's put an asterisk beside his name for not interested."

"Okay, Your Grace, will do."

"Then another said "who's next?"

Sitting back and holding her list she said "I have only one choice on my list and that's Queen Marsha of Greenland." Then she waited to hear any comments and there were none so she continued to say "the way she and I worked together to handle the situation of the Sorentito uprising was impressive. Never once did she question my authority or become a coward at any time."

Then a couple from the team chose one speaker and that one said "we remember and she was a pleasure to work with during those trying times."

Daisy stood up and said "unless anyone has another candidate then I make a motion that we start the process to prepare her for the position." With no objections she then said "then this meeting is adjourned so go and enjoy the next two days."

Knowing that this decision was not permanent she asked to speak with her great grand moms tonight. Talking with her husband and just enjoying being home again this night. To be selfish is something she never considered before but talking with him she said "you know we have been working a long time and we now know that we are leaving within a year…"

He cut her off and said "do you want to retire?"

A big laugh seemed to just jump out of her when she said "yes both of us need to retire!"

"Your wish is my command, or are you using your Master Vagan mind tricks on me?"

"Always dear, I'm always using my tricks."

This got a laugh from them both and after some fun in bed she went to sleep very happy about tomorrow. Deep in blissful sleep she then hears "Daisy wake-up."

"Wake-up I'm deep in sleep…"

Then Shasha says to her "just wake-up dear for this dream within a dream with us. Now what is your request to see us tonight?"

"I would like to discuss with you my replacement as the High Councilor on the Earth."

Shasha said "okay let's ask Seliah to visit us to do that."

"Good idea dear, she's on her way now" Tamla said.

Daisy then spent some time at her new home that she and Rick picked out before. While there they prepared for Seliah's visit and discussed the things that she and Rick will do there on Millennia. She didn't want to tell them about all the things that have happened on Earth because it would need to be repeated when Seliah arrived.

Just as the kettle on the stove started to whistle, Seliah was there in the kitchen. Then Daisy said "grandma, how did you do that?"

"Easy my girl, it's all about controlling energy."

Both of her moms hugged her and Shasha said "Brenda, oops, I mean Seliah, how are you doing?"

Seliah smiled at her and said "I'm doing great mom, learning all I can from my Chief."

Watching Shasha be the mother that she is, Tamla said "okay we called you here to discuss something with Daisy."

While looking Seliah right in the eyes, Daisy said "grandma I want to find a replacement for me as the High Councilor on Earth…"

As she took a breath Seliah asked "is this because you know you will be coming here within a year?"

"Yes it is so Rick and I have decided to retire and just fade away."

Tamla then said "we liked her idea of being proactive and finding a replacement now."

Shasha nodded her head and said "we thought it would be good to hear your thoughts since you held that position before Daisy did."

"Well thank you both for considering me, I know Daisy has been visiting you here for a while now. It makes sense she would contact you so now let's hear who you've decided on Daisy?"

"Well grandma I don't know if you followed what has been happening on Earth lately, but let me fill you in just in case you've missed anything. First we broke the world up into seven continents each governed by a king or queen. They would all follow the laws of the new Human government. North America which we've continued to have problems with as you know later decided to revolt. Seeing this slowly happening through their government we went into action. Upon that we had a meeting with the leader of this new government they named Sorentito and I know that's familiar to you especially from before you left."

Tamla said "wow so what was the plan?"

"The plan was to recognize that we were going to lose North America. With this knowledge we negotiated with their leader King Jarod to allow the people there that wanted to leave some time to do so. He agreed, and as Queen Marsha was preparing to do so, Jarod started amassing an army, and then he moved on the palace."

Now Shasha said "okay Daisy take a breath and then continue."

"Thanks, now to make a long story short Queen Marsha worked with me to save them from this attack. Her leadership was amazing, she was the perfect one to handle the situation and we were successful. Since then we relocated her people to the island of Greenland and she has been our protection from King Jerod."

Seliah disappeared for a few minutes then returned and said "well there is no one in your linage to take your place right now. So you have the right to name your successor, plus Queen Marsha has received the approval from the High Councilor Daanic."

Tamla and Shasha were both in agreement with the new High Councilor of Earth. Wanting to wake up and get started on preparing Marsha for her promotion, this was all Daisy could think about. Then looking at Seliah she asked "will she be part of this universal hierarchy?"

"I'm afraid not. That will go to the next one in our linage" then Seliah disappeared.

Standing there kind of sad Daisy asked "why did she leave like that, without saying goodbye?"

Tamla said "who knows maybe she was called back for an emergency?"

With that said, Daisy woke up, and noticed Rick was still in bed. She looked over at the clock and it read 5:55! Wow, I guess I didn't need that much sleep. Then rolling over she told him that she was going to walk to the lake, and then gave him a kiss.

He said "do you want me to come with you?"

Leaning over she kissed him and said "I would love that."

Off they went downstairs to the kitchen to make tea for their walk to the lake. The moon was still out without a cloud the night sky looked like a very large city with all the stars sparkling. With her travels still fresh she wanted to tell him everything they talked about. In the light of the moon these two worked out what they wanted to do with the rest of their time on Earth.

CHAPTER 20

Greenland, yes it's cold, but it's also a peaceful place with Queen Marsha ruling, and why wouldn't it be. But all that is going to change soon and she doesn't know that yet. This announcement came two days ago that the High Councilor Daisy was planning a visit, now that day has arrived, and everything is ready for them to come.

She decided to travel by boat because this time of year it's way too pretty to fly. Marsha always looked forward to a visit from her friend, who is also the High Councilor. There Marsha stood watching the very large and fast ships pull into the dock. The security detail unloaded first to secure the area, then her Grace walked down the platform right to Queen Marsha. Daisy looked at her and then Marsha said "is there something wrong Your Grace?"

"Nothing at all, I'm so happy to see you again, and we do have business to discuss."

Marsha was never told what this business was about, as they were driving to the palace up on this most beautiful mountain range for many kilometers, she asked her what this was about and Daisy said "all in due time dear just relax."

Keeping her in suspense wasn't done on purpose, but Daisy wanted to spring the news to her at the right moment. It was too early for dinner so Daisy asked her to show her some of the new businesses that had sprung up since her last visit. This took them up to the dinner hour and Daisy wanted some of their famous seafood tonight with some white wine. Just small talk at the dinner table and then Daisy rushed her off to her chambers where they could talk alone.

"What a day it's been" Daisy said after only the tea and cookies were left for them.

"Yes it has been Your Grace. I so enjoy being with you, now will you tell me what's going on?"

Putting her hands in hers she looked her square in the eyes and said "Marsha there is not another person on this planet that I trust more than you, you know this don't you?"

"I do now Your Grace, but trust with what?"

Daisy said "to guide our planet, my friend."

Now that Daisy made it clear to her, she still couldn't believe this and said "but what about your assistant, Your Grace wouldn't she be the logical choice?"

"Normally that would be ideal, because she is a wonderful assistant, and if something happened to me she would fill in very nicely. Here's the conundrum, I don't want that to happen, I want to choose my successor now before I retire."

"How much time will I have to transition into this position?"

Jumping up Daisy said "great so you'll do it?"

"Your Grace I wouldn't say no to you, even if you asked me to be the royal dog catcher."

The ladies were both excited about the same thing but for different reasons. They sat there for a few minutes just taking it all in, and then Daisy remembered the question she asked her, so she said "I would like to retire in four weeks. That is two weeks for you to finish up here and then two weeks for me to train you. Will that be enough time for you to work things out?"

"I will do that for you Your Grace, thank you for considering me it's an honor."

"It's all my honor, my Queen and I'll see myself out. Let's have breakfast in the morning before I leave."

The transition went over well, Marsha was able to pick her successor and Greenland now has a king named George for their ruler. Earth has a new High Councilor named Marsha. Daisy and Rick are traveling to the planet Millennia two to three times a week to prepare for the move.

Back on the farm Daisy told Rick her plan "since we've spent a lifetime giving and certainly plenty of receiving. I would like to really go all out and spend each day doing something to help others by using my own two hands."

"Darling I will do anything you want to do, and I like your idea, so let's make it happen."

For the next few days they did a lot of research and found many things to be involved in. One thing they did first was to have more money automatically go to some select charities and then they contacted their lawyer to have her put these charities in their will.

Rick liked a program where these doctors would travel the world and give free medical services. So to support him in doing that, she decided that they would go there together. Her job in this was to help with the administration department, where she can use her many contacts to acquire much needed supplies. For them these were a very fulfilling three months spent and after this they moved on to do something else.

Their astral visits to Millennia were very promising now that they were free to give more of themselves while still on Earth. Daisy spent some time at the Wizard's castle learning all about being a doctor and a wizard, while Rick would learn from Tamla all about governing. After work even though it was a dream they would always have dinner at Shasha's restaurant.

Today was starting as wonderful as could be there on the farm. She awoke with nothing but gratitude flowing from her and it seemed to be more than normal. For some reason Rick asked her if she felt like today was going to be a special day for them. They found that they were both in agreement that something special would happen today.

During their visits with Tamla and Shasha they learned some very interesting things. One of them was finding out that they will be with them soon, and this was very important. Daisy asked if Marsha will have any connection with her through dreams and was told no. This was a bit disturbing to her and when Seliah would visit her, she would help her with this concern.

Rick didn't really have any problems with leaving Earth, well maybe just a little one, leaving the winery would be hard. Often when he and Daisy talked about that, he would act really sad, and then laugh when he remembered about how Barbara their oldest took it over many years ago.

Their son being a very specialized military man was so successful, that he made it all the way to become the General of the Army. This meant he didn't have time to meet someone, so he never married, and therefore had no children. Only the daughters are married with children and both built homes on their farm. Paul made an agreement with his parents that he would live on the base in the officer's quarters, but they would let him keep his room in their home.

Going outside today they planned on doing a tour around the farm and leaving their memories in many places that over the years were special to them. Barbara was working in the winery and she wanted dad to taste a new blend that she told him about before planting the grapes. She took what he had learned from great grandpa Brad to an even higher level. Daisy loved watching them geek out over these beautiful grapes and she enjoyed tasting the wine.

They then strolled around the fields looking for a few fresh vegetables to pick and also leaving their memories in those places. The family that was hired to work the farm many years ago bought a parcel of the land and built a home on it. Now these people were just like family, both Rick and Daisy left them something also. After visiting with them, showing them the area of land that they are going to will to them, they then left their memories there also.

Several other places they would stop at and leave their memories behind and last but not least was the lake. There Daisy made so many memories with Brenda, Brad, Gloria, Marsha, Rick and all her children. Now they will make some last ones here again, they are going to be some that she and Rick will take with them to Millennia. Leaving the gazebo and walking around the lake hand in hand Rick said "I am so happy today, because now I am conscious that we will be together after leaving this world."

Listening to him talk all she could do was reflect on how they met and what a wonderful life on this planet they've had.

She wanted to talk but, right now just walking, breathing, and holding his hand was more than enough. Then seeing several birds fly by he thought they might by falcons and said "look isn't this earth beautiful, but unlike Millennia which is literally beyond this world."

As they turned the last corner before going back to the gazebo, she said "I agree with everything you've said and we are so lucky for sure. Let's go sit down. I'd like to write another song."

"Sounds exciting, I feel like walking back to the lake, and skipping some rocks."

"Boys gotta love them, have fun" she then got comfortable and opened her tablet.

My Love

This world feels unkind without him
He makes me smile in spite of them

These many days of happiness and joy
He treats me like I was his favorite toy

To find love is to cherish even more
Once realized then you do the score

Living together on grandpa's farm
A great place to be safe and warm

Thinking and writing for heaven's sake
That's where you'd find me at the lake

He and grandpa grew grapes for wine
Bottled them up to drink at another time

This song is about the man I dearly love
Heals with his hands as soft as a dove

Walking back after noticing that she was finished writing Rick approached her and said "are you finished?"

"Yes do you want to read it?"

"Sure who's it about?"

"You tell me" then she handed him the tablet.

As he read this he quickly realized that she was talking about him. Wiping a tear or two from his eyes, he felt so honored that this important woman, who, at one time led the whole world, would think this much about him. Kissing her on the forehead he said "that was beautiful, thank you so much. I love you."

Heading back home they were walking in step, with their arms around each other, and just loving nature. Their grandchildren were playing outside and this was a wonderful site for them. Stopping by for hugs and to tell them how much they loved them all. Going up the steps into the door and waiting for them at the table were their children Barbara, Paul and Cleo.

Before Rick or Daisy could say anything Paul said "mom, dad, we need to go into town."

Daisy said "Okay son, what is this for?"

"Something to do with your will I believe. Your lawyer called and said she needs to see you both today."

Rick then grabbed his phone and said "I'll call her and let her know we're on our way."

She responded and said "great make sure you bring your deed to the home."

Looking over at Daisy he just shrugged his shoulders and said "I'll go and get it while you get ready."

"Okay."

Getting in the car, Daisy and Rick drove off to the courthouse. Waiting about ten minutes after they left, all three siblings had their children loaded, and ready to leave. Driving and discussing how wonderful this day has been Rick said to her "I wonder what this need for the deed is about? When I asked her she said she was with another client and couldn't talk right now."

"Probably some missing numbers or maybe they need another official copy."

"Well I guess we'll… What in the world is going on?" he said this as they turned the corner towards the courthouse.

Then they both noticed a huge banner over the road, which read "Celebrating our favorite Family."

As they turned into the parking lot and parked the car. They noticed a mob coming toward then in party gear and balloons. Almost afraid to get out of the car, they did, and the crowd shouted "welcome to your retirement party!"

They picked them both up and carried them to the big stand in front of the courthouse, where their lawyer was waiting for them. By the time Daisy got up there she looked at her and said "and to think you were part of this little rouse."

Shortly after their family arrived, that's when the whole celebration started. The kids ran around in the park with their friends and there were plenty of amusements for them to play in too. The kids were out of earshot. Then the speakers lined up ready to go, one after another. Many gave speeches, either for Daisy or Rick, and then the new High Councilor Marsha went last.

She was so beautiful walking up to the podium, Daisy was so proud that she was her friend. She was then announced as the High Councilor Marsha. Waiting for the crowd to settle down, so when they were quiet, and they gave her their attention, she spoke.

"My fellow Humans, I am here to speak about High Councilor Daisy. There are many wonderful things said about her here today and I wouldn't attempt to try to top them. What I do want to tell you is how much of a friend she is, and how much she believed in me is beyond my ability to thank her properly."

Looking the crowd over, she took a deep breath, and then continued. *"Let me share one of the most important times that her courage and leadership were beyond reproach. This was when my kingdom of North America was falling into an insurrection of the worst kind. She took all the information that she had and took quick decisive action. Her plan of taking quick action, even in the face of trickery from our enemy, saved many lives, and treasure. I can't really add to this story which to me defines her greatness so I will close and say thank you High Councilor Daisy for being my light, mentor and most of all, my friend."*

She received a very long and loud round of applause for her speech. Daisy and Rick were both called up to receive a plaque and to unveil their busts for city hall. Rick spoke first at the request of Daisy and he talked about how wonderful it was to grow up in Otium. He mentioned many of his friends at the hospital and his private practice. When he finished he said "thank you all, my fellow good people of Otium. When the world needed help you were there."

Never to outshine her wonderful man, Daisy gave him a hug, and told him she loves him. Then walking up to the podium, moving the microphone down, she threw out kisses to the crowd. She proceeded to tell how much she loved them all and they then told her that they loved her too. In conclusion of her speech this is what she said "Otium and all of you will always have a place in my heart." For the people of Otium that's a great place to be.

After many hugs and tears especially from Daisy and Rick, because this might be the last time they see many of their friends again in this lifetime. However they did walk down and enjoy all of the day's festivities. Feeling so complete from the day's long and glorious activities they were ready for sleep.

Walking in the door the first thing Rick said was "I'm getting a shower and going to bed do you want to join me?"

She smiled winked and then said "just get the water warm and I'll be there soon enough."

This night was so blissful for them, it was spring, the wind was warm coming in, and they were so into feeling each other's touch. Their shower was memorable with back cleaning, lots of kisses all over and then taken their passion to the bed. The last thing she said was "ah."

No astral travel tonight, even though it was on the schedule, her great grandma's decided to cancel it, and let them rest. Knowing they still had another big day tomorrow.

Daanic seemed very anxious today and the reason was clear, she knew it was time in her heart to leave the council. The problem was how to tell Seliah without others finding out or being suspicious. Going to her chambers she summoned Seliah to meet her later on that day. Then when her granddaughter Seliah approached, she said "we need to talk."

"I figured that much Your Grace, what would you like to talk about?"

The room was empty except for them and Daanic said "this is about your ascension to my position soon."

"I'm confused I thought I would have to work my way up like you did Your Grace."

"It doesn't always work that way and you are ready. We've known this for some time, plus I need to move on."

"But what about Jenny, Tamla, or Shasha, aren't they next in line?"

"They are going to do other things, and Jenny will stay on to help you."

"That will be great she knows a lot."

"Yes she does, and I like knowing that she will be there to help you."

Not thinking of herself, Seliah asked Daanic "what about Daisy, will she take my place on the council?"

She laughed and said "my granddaughter, don't forget she needs to spend time on Millennia."

"That is so true, and my moms are looking forward to that. I guess she will move here in due time." Then as if she forgot what she was told she asked "where are you going after I take over?"

"I'm not sure, I suppose I will transform into a dragon just like the Councilors before did."

And so she did change to become a most beautiful dragon, along with her new teacher Jillela, who herself was ready to become an alicorn soon. Who knows what Ella will transform into next probably a sun or a planet with rings around her.

Working with people was always Daisy's forte and helping them was Rick's purpose in life. What a combination these two are when they put their talents together. Especially when they are 100 percent directed into doing good things for others and today that's just what they were doing.

This time they decided to travel south and help their fellow Humans of South America. Who were suffering from some wide spread flooding that recently happened. Rick worked in their hospitals with patients of a type of malaria from the recent large new mosquito population. With a lot of the infrastructure destroyed by the massive flooding, Daisy pitched in to help organize the world relief to repair them.

In one of the hospitals that Rick was helping in a five year old boy was wondering around lost. Finishing up with a patient he spotted him outside his room and in the lobby. Fortunately the workload of patients was very low today so Rick stepped out and approached him. Kneeling down and making eye contact Rick said "what's your name? Mine is Rick" he told him.

The little boy had been crying and when he stopped he was so choked up so badly that Rick didn't understand him. With that problem he quickly decided what to do and carefully standing up he took the little boys hand. After that his crying started to diminish then Rick said "come with me I have a surprise for you."

One of the nurses noticed this and said "what are you doing Dr. Brackett?"

"Just taking care of one of my patients, who I think needs some good medicine." The little boy didn't quite understand this but continued to walk with Dr. Rick anyway.

Turning the corner, walking outside, it now seemed more apparent what was happening, when this little crying boy spotted the big ice cream cone sign about ten meters away. Before Rick could do or say anything his hand was dropped and this little boy ran to the counter. A bigger smile Rick hadn't seen in a long time and his heart pounded with approval.

After they each had their ice cream Rick took his hand again. Finding one of the local officials he told him that this little boy was lost and to please update him when they found his family. After returning back to the hospital the nurses and a couple of doctors asked if he found the little boys home. Sadly

Rick said "no but I told the official I left him with to update me when they do."

All the while Daisy was at least ten kilometers away working on repairing a bridge. She really enjoyed taking charge, especially pulling in some favors to get materials, and expert help to do this. This bridge had one of its embankments pulled out so the decision that was made from the Corp of Engineers was to span it with a metal roller bridge. This was to be done by some engineers flown in from Europe that specialized in this.

Once they arrived she asked them what they needed. They then made a list of the bridge materials, quickly she got on the phone, made many calls, and one was to her son the General of the Army. The materials will be flown there within two days, now they could start preparing the ground, and strengthening the river banks where the new bridge will sit. Shortly after that, it was getting late, so she returned to her temporary home.

Eating dinner and sipping some of the bottled wine that Barbara had perfected they were still excited about the day. She told him about the bridge and how well Paul came through for her. Then after enjoying listening to her talk about all the heavy bridge materials that were coming in he took a breath. She smiled at him and said "what?"

A little laugh and he said "well I can't compete with that, but I did help a little five year old boy find his home, and along the way we both enjoyed some ice cream." Then he took a long sip of wine.

Her smile had turned into tears, they were the wettest kind, and they are the happy ones. She said "you are so sweet, I don't know if I deserve you."

Tonight they will travel back to Millennia and spend some time in their home, there he will walk her around the lake, and then both will look forward to eating some of the most delicious fruits ever tasted by Earthlings.

Spending time with Tamla and Shasha at dinner Rick said "this wine is very good, but just wait until my Barbara comes up here, and starts working with it. She will make it even better, I can guarantee you that."

Putting her hand on his Shasha said "I would love to have her work with me in my restaurant."

Sitting and talking about the day's events that were shared by all and enjoying the time. Daisy talked about being a wizard when she arrived there permanently and she thought that would be a good change. The one area she was becoming more interested in was engineering, especially the planning part of it. Tamla liked listening to her excitement and said "I think you will like the castle I remember how much Brenda and Brad did."

For Rick wasn't sure about leaving Earth, after the help he provided today to the people. Talking about how he could learn from Tamla he started to entertain another thought. Looking over at Shasha he asked her "would it be okay if I spent some off time working in your restaurant?"

This made her smile and she said "I would love to have you in the restaurant. What would you like to do there?"

"I'm not sure, maybe do some cooking, but I wouldn't be opposed to helping in whatever needs done."

"Now that's a great way to be and it's good to learn all aspects of the restaurant."

They spent a few more minutes talking and sharing some urban stories back and forth. Rick and Daisy were really beginning to dig the idea of going to Millennia soon, but both admitted that their lives are very satisfying right now on Earth. Shasha and

Tamla both told them how proud they are of the work that they are doing there.

Just as Shasha was finishing a thought to them, they woke up, and Daisy lay there for a few minutes until Rick walked out of the bathroom, and said "sugar, are you going to wake up?"

"Yes I am, what did you think about our dream last night?"

"Very interesting, I wasn't sure if we were coming back here again or not?"

They stayed there on the farm another week and then returned to Otium to have another family reunion.

CHAPTER 21

Was it meant to be? Why did consciousness just start to leave the Earth? What is happening now that Daisy and Rick have left the planet? Marsha is now growing tired and this is disturbing. The new High Councilor of the Pleaides is Seliah, Daanic is now a dragon named Athena, and Tamla still is the High Councilor on Millennia. Daisy is an understudy of Tamla, so that she can follow in her family's lineage. In the Wizard's castle Rick is geeking out over his love of science just like Daisy's grandparents did before.

The Master Vagans are gone and the king of Sorentito is constantly trying to conquer South America. It is taking many resources from the Human kingdom to prevent that from happening. Marsha misses Daisy so much, wishes she could just contact her again, but she doesn't have that connection through her dreams, and is confined to Earths dimensions.

The Earth's economies are growing, especially in certain areas of Earth that are predominately in the Human kingdom. Recently the Human kingdom was split into several nations, but they still are governed by the High Council, for when an emergency arises, and one was about to.

These Earth cycles always go in the same direction, in that there are booms and busts, war, and peace. Many centuries have passed and the Human kingdom has disappeared into a long forgotten history. Daisy is the High Councilor on Millennia, Tamla and Shasha are both chief elders on the High Council of the Pleaides. Rick continues to grow in becoming a wizard at their castle and is now one of their chiefs.

With no contact from the Pleaides, or the planet Millennia, Earth has been left to go it on her own, very much like the dark ages from before. They haven't done a very good job with their civilization, so there have been wars and famines for many years in between the ones of plenty. The leaders of the world have decided that they can't manage without an occasional war economy to keep them in power.

This war economy has been written about by the true economists who've said over and over that nothing good can come of it. When the powers that be would try and operate without a war they would start out good until greed would get the best of them. Once they discovered another one of them cheating in many of the same ways they did, they would become indignant.

Most of the people in the world are peaceful, but when the ones in power would want to stop the other from cheating, they would then quickly drag the people down with them. They would beat the war drums with some manufactured excuse to go to war, but never fighting to win, and rarely to conquer any territory. What they did do was to loan out money to the nations they were in, so the governments could then build their war machines, and owe them a financial debt.

Seeing this happening from the heavens did cause much despair, but they knew that it was necessary to apply pressure on the Spirits to cause them to shine like diamonds. This day will come in the future to harvest those jewels because they are only there on Earth to shine. Contemplating this was a new beautiful dragon named Athena, who wrote this telling song;

Diamonds

Precious souls who come into this world
Separated by flags of hate to be unfurled
Blessed these souls come from heaven
To love and not fly away as the raven

Diamonds hardened by pressure
They sparkle like golden treasure
With brilliant light to shine

Finding fault in none they sparkle for all
They who were chosen to answer the call
Being here for all to show them the way
Chosen to come now we hear them say

Diamonds hardened by pressure
They sparkle like golden treasure
With brilliant light to shine

Through hate, fear and judgement they'll be
Purified by shining their lights for all to see
The light of love gives strength to overcome
Things done wrong will then be over thrown

Diamonds hardened by pressure

They sparkle like golden treasure
With brilliant light to shine

During the time the heavens watched the Earth being destroyed by hate. The wars were now to become worldwide and the powers that are felt that they would win. Without the knowledge that no one wins in fighting any war they continued with their plans.

Europeans were building ships, planes and tanks for what they say is the defense of their nations. While the people of Asia noticed this build-up, they became fearful of being attacked. They then in turn bought into these fears and built up their military to match Europe's force. Both nations did this for several years and during that time they borrowed large amounts of money. By borrowing this money to build the military they brought on their people a terrible depression.

Humane projects that would help their people were put on hold and then the government's leaders would blame the other nation for threatening them with their military build-ups. Athena watched on from the Pleaides and was so sad to see her people suffer.

The leaders had backed themselves into a corner, and the nations of Asia were getting ready to vote. These leaders couldn't undo what they had done to create such animosity that the people felt toward them. In secret these leaders went to the money powers of the world, and asked them what could be done for to win back the people. They were then given more money so they could essentially buy these elections. With these loans there was only one thing required from them.

Eastern Europe is very lovely this time of year with all the flowers blooming and the trees coming back to life. That is until it was noticed that in the northwest corner of Asia there was a large military build-up. The leaders in Europe now are making plans to defend against an invasion there.

After a few weeks, still no invasion, then with no warning or even a sign of a build-up, the forces from Asia attacked southern Europe from Africa. This was a surprise because the last time they looked at the Nation of Africa there were no large forces there. It was later determined that the force in the north were mostly decoys and that the leader of Asia had secretly made a deal with the leader of Africa through their mutual wealthy war investors.

War was now something different than in the days of the Human kingdoms, it is now mechanical, and very inhumane. Killing is to be done on a large scale with no apparent purpose other than to conquer territory. Now the Asian armies have a foothold in southern Europe, are to bring in supplies to reinforce their numbers, and are planning to move north and east.

The Europeans are now scrambling to bring forces south to stop the further aggression of their enemy. While this is happening the Asian military is now forming to move into the north side of Europe. Seeing this enemy movement, the European Generals have decided to invade Asia, right in between where the enemy is now located in the south, and where they are preparing to attack in the north. This is a classic move to shift forces and then attack an aggressive enemy where they are the most vulnerable.

One thing for sure is that this war will last only a couple of years, until both sides hold the ground that they have conquered, then and call a truce. There will be peace for several years until North America invades South America and moves all the way east to the Atlantic coast. The leaders in Africa took notice of this and have begun to strengthen their fortifications in their northwest area. They felt that North America might send ships to those ports and invade soon. All the while the world's wealthy investors will loan money for these military endeavors.

Leaders of these nations would borrow and borrow, then once in a while raise taxes, and fane paying down these debts. Then all the while all they did was put financial shackles on their people. All the while the rich got richer and many more middle class people were made poor. In the scheme of things even when the people would elect new leaders this cycle of borrowing and taxing never did end.

In the world there where some wealthy people that started to become conscious of these facts, even though they didn't have the power to stop it, at least they tried to help the people. What they would do was form groups to pull their finances together, use those resources to feed, clothe, and help the poor of the world. This wasn't easy and they couldn't help everyone but they did shine and make a difference where ever they went.

A few nations formed a loose axis alliance to attempt and conquer a large part of the free world. These are the nations where their people are free to elect the leaders, they have freedom to speak, and could keep most of their earnings or inventions.

The newly formed axis alliance was ruled by dictators and their people had little freedom. In so that these people did not produce much in wealth or riches, and therefore the dictators wanted to take what the free nations owned.

The Asian forces in southern Europe were building and building a larger army. European leaders knew what this meant and they once again started to build their forces up too meet this threat. The leader of Europe sent a message to the Asian dictator asking to negotiate a peace treaty. Word came back that they could meet at a neutral nation, so they both picked Australia.

This meeting was going well, for both sides expressed an interest in not having another war. The leader from Europe expressed a concern for their economies and how the people were suffering. One of the things the leader from Asia asked for was that Europe would withdraw their forces from west central Asia. Now this was a start of negotiations, thought the leader of Europe, and she then asked for his removal of forces from her southern border.

Needless to say this meeting did not continue when the Asian dictator pounded his hand on the table and said "we will not give up our conquered territories! If you want peace then you will submit to my demands only."

Her only response was "go to hell, you moron." Then she left with her people.

Elsewhere in the world the North American army that was occupying half of South America was planning to conquer the rest of the continent. Knowing that they did not have the ability to prevent their enemy from conquering them, the South American leader made a bold move and contacted the leader of Europe. This meeting was held in Greenland and a rescue plan was created.

Flying under the radar were these European planes that took off in the middle of the night. Flying across the Atlantic Ocean, then southward to their destination, which will be South America. The people there were loaded onto commercial planes, while their precious belongings and equipment were loaded onto these very large cargo jets.

The mission was a success and now the leaders, the wealthy, the leading scientists, and many of the middle class people of South America are now in Europe. The leader of South America managed to evacuate most of his military after the civilians were safe and in the air.

At his time the world was split into three camps at war; these were North America, Europe with some from South America, and then with Africa and Asia together. North America stayed out of the fighting between Europe and the African/Asian force for the most part. Their border with Africa was safe in Brazil and Europe didn't seem to want to attack from Greenland. Although the Americans did have plans to take Greenland in the future.

Several months went by and Europe fell to the African/Asian forces. Europe did ask North America for help, but they didn't seem to want to be involved with the battle at this time. They did buy Greenland from them for some military equipment to help in their battle in Eastern Europe.

Soon after Asia and Africa split up the continent of Europe up between them, did the Americans attack North Africa, Eastern Asia, and Iceland all at the same time. These attacks were very forceful and concentrated. Being weakened from conquering Europe, the African/Asian force couldn't hold the Americans back!

New boundaries were drawn and because the American gamble didn't pay off the war wouldn't end there. The Asian/African alliance soon regrouped and started another offensive. This time it was to take back the land they had previously conquered. What they didn't know was the main reason the Americans attacked so quickly was to capture several advanced physicists from Otium.

The Americans pulled out of those captured territories and the Asian/African alliance couldn't understand why. They just took the land back and believed that the Americans were just afraid of their mighty army. Years went by and the Otium physicists they captured were performing well in their studies, and then one day it happened!

A meeting is called, the chiefs are hurrying to their positions and Leto is ready to announce. "Fellow Pleiadians please stand for her Grace Seliah the High Councilor."

Walking to her seat on the podium she looked left and right and smiled at all her friends in the Council. Reaching the steps she very deliberately walked up and then once behind the podium turned around and said "please be seated."

No one knew what this was about except for her and her staff. The chiefs and elders in the Council were still moving around asking each other what was going on. Then she raised her hand and when they saw her do this they soon became quiet. Reaching back with her hand Seliah motioned for Jenny to join her at the podium. Walking up with a document under her arm Jenny did just that. Very quietly she said "Your Grace do you want me to give the report?"

"No my dear I will do that, just stand here next to me please."

Jenny handed her the document and then put her hands together in front. Looking around and nodding Seliah could see that the Council was starting to get nervous, so she then gave this message;

"We are now faced with some disturbing news from Earth. This isn't the normal news about them attacking each other or going to war. Those issues we have dealt with many times before. The report we have been given is that the Americans have with the help of several Otium physicists developed and tested an atomic weapon."

She put the report down and then just looked around noticing the silent faces in front of her. Taking a deep breath she picked up the report again, folding the pages neatly, she then put them back into the folder, and handed them back to Jenny. She gave Jenny a half smile then turned to Leto, and said "do we need to follow the same plan that the great Paul Miller, Margret Brown and some 144,000 others so bravely volunteered for many ages ago?"

Leto picked up this same book again, and said "I'm afraid we do Your Grace."

CHAPTER 22

Where, oh where, do those dragons and alicorns live? That was the question that Seliah wanted to ask them the next time they would visit the High Council of the Pleiades. Surprisingly they didn't show up for her coronation as the new High Councilor. She was a little sad but understood that the former High Councilors have moved on.

The boats are out today to take advantage of the new moon from the night before. It is believed that when there is a new moon the fish will be near the top of the water looking for food the next morning. Each day is different for these simple people in this peaceful little village. The huts are small and each is occupied by just one person.

One of the villagers named Paul was talking with his friend Cory about the disappearances of Ambrosia, Elizabeth and Margo. He said "where do they go when we don't see them out fishing or tending their gardens, and sometimes they are gone for days?"

"Paul, that's just what I was wondering, it is very strange because they always seem to be taken care of, even if they miss days of catching fish?"

The villagers are pretty much independent of each other. They fish, plant crops, gather wood and make their own clothes. Since doing these chores which tend to occupy most of their day, by evening time they are more than ready for sleep.

No one remembers their former lives, except the few who turn into dragons, and alicorns. Although when these dragons and alicorns do return, they don't remember even being gone, just waking up from a long sleep. Ambrosia, Margo and Elizabeth are a little different than the rest in that whatever they catch, grow or create is shared between each other.

Paul ran into Elizabeth during today, after she was not seen for days, so he asked her "where have you been Elizabeth?"

Looking rather puzzled she said "I didn't know was I gone. Maybe I was asleep for a few days."

Not being sure if she was telling the truth or not he said "okay, maybe you were just very tired. Do you need any fish or vegetables?"

"No we're fine, for some reason we have enough."

"Who is this *we* you are talking about?"

"I'm including Margo and Ambrosia with me. Now stop interrogating me" Then she walked on and didn't look back.

None here are married, without children, and they all seemed to be around a perfect age of growth, probably around 33. With all of them working to take care of only themselves, the planet provided them with just enough fish, and produce to survive without being spoiled. Where is this beautiful planet you might ask? Well it's not far at all from where the humans are trying to destroy this same planet.

So what's the difference? First these villagers are in a place known as the garden, which is in a different dimension known as the fifth, this place was written about before, and it does exist. Souls left this place many eons ago and are now traveling back. After many incarnations lived on Earth they come back to the knowledge of nothingness.

Paradise is such a dreamy word and it can mean many different things to each of us. Here in Eden which is a most beautiful garden, there is the truest definition of the word. There are no machines to make noise, or to "do the work of ten men." Money is not used or any form of currency, although sometimes the villagers do like to barter with each other, and this seems to be really just a means of communication. Love is not a word that comes in vogue because hate is never shown.

Paul and Cory are best buddies, they aren't aware of what that means, and neither do they care. Since they unintentionally built their huts next to each other, and seemed to share the same common knowledge of fishing, friendship was only natural. Many of the villagers became close merely because of their vicinity to one another.

The girls had a different reason for being close, but none of them knew why. Somehow they were each led individually up this mountain to an area secluded from the rest. In settling in this area, they learned that they were neighbors, and soon became good friends. Today they started to drift a little off from the normal way of just tending to your own needs.

Elizabeth was talking with them about her conversation with Paul. She said "you know Paul stopped me the other day and asked where I went off to for days. I told him that I just slept for those days and then he asked me if I had enough food since I didn't work those days. I slipped and told him that we seem to have provisions when we awake."

Margo said "so you included us in this?"

"Yes, I'm sorry it just slipped."

Ambrosia just stood there listening and thinking about the implications of this. Luckily the village people are not organized into groups or governments to become fearful of each other. Even though these ladies did remember their past, they wouldn't remember becoming alicorns, and travelling into the third or fourth dimension. They did have a higher knowledge apart from the rest in the village.

For now they didn't have any problems with Paul and Cory's questions about where they would go to. Especially since these ladies didn't know if they even went anywhere. Until something changes to enlighten them this will just have to be a mystery.

Waiting for Elizabeth and Margo to work out those questions from Paul, Ambrosia then said "can one of you catch a fish for me tomorrow and another pick up some vegetables for me?"

Margo said "sure I can bring you back a fish."

"Thanks."

Elizabeth said "okay I found a good spot for produce, so I'll bring back plenty. Why do you need this done?"

"My shoes are getting worn, and I need to find some materials to make a new pair."

Looking at her shoes Margo had an idea "could you make me a pair too?"

Laughing Elizabeth then said "wait a minute, its common knowledge that I make the best pair of shoes."

Ambrosia thought for a minute and said "you do make the best shoes and your clothes hold up pretty well too. Would you make the shoes for us while I catch the fish?"

They both looked at Margo, and then she said to them "okay I like picking, cleaning and preparing the produce. How about I take care of that tomorrow?"

Later in the next day the girls were together at Elizabeth's hut trying on their new shoes. Into the kitchen they then went and Margo started preparing the produce. She had lettuce, tomatoes, mushrooms and onions. Ambrosia went outside to check on the fire she had started and then to cook the fish she caught that day. Elizabeth was the host so she prepared the table and poured the wine she had made before.

Ambrosia lifted her glass and said "this is a great idea we came up with."

They clicked their glasses together and all agreed. Maybe it was the wine or just the fact that these good friends have stumbled onto a new idea that will change their world? Whatever it was, it brought them together, and to sing this new song they came up with.

Working Together

Life is a beautiful thing when you discern
That working as one people you will learn
How wonderful things are for all to see
All part of the magic that is you and me

All the ah of working together
Something to share we bring
Of ourselves the music to sing

You cook the fish and I'll sew the shoes
These are chores we share of these clues
Alone is no place that we want to live
Make sure to spend your time to give

All the ah of working together
Something to share we bring
Of ourselves the music to sing

In conclusion this is our song we sing
To all joy and happiness we will bring
Seeing all the lights in the sky at night
Proves to us that together is just right

All the ah of working together
Something to share we bring
Of ourselves the music to sing

ABOUT THE AUTHOR

Kelly Fields was born in 1962 and moved to Florida from Texas at three. After high school he joined the Army as a Combat Engineer and a Paratrooper in the 82nd Airborne Div. He has been married for over 29 years and has worked in the engineering field as a CAD engineer for over 33 years. He wrote his first book 'Avant-garde, A Boom Generation' in 2015 and the sequel 'Millennium Earth' in 2016. This is the last of the trilogy of A Boom Generation series. Hopefully a movie will be made of them in the future.